"Why do you want me back, Rad?"

His reply was instant and sharp. "Why do you think?"

"I don't know." Lainie's eyes blurred. "Maybe you want revenge against me. I know I hurt and disappointed you all those years ago. I also know that you still want me physically...." Her voice trembled and she steeled herself to remain composed.

"You're a very clever girl, Lainie, to figure it out all by yourself," he sneered. "Or were you about to add something? Were you going to suggest that I might be desperately in love with you?"

She shook her head slowly. Rad didn't love her. He never had. And once he got his revenge—or tired of her—what then? She couldn't bear to be without him again!

JANET DAILEY AMERICANA

AFTER THE STORM

Harlequin Books

TORONTO • NEW YORK • LONDON
AMSTERDAM • PARIS • SYDNEY • HAMBURG
STOCKHOLM • ATHENS • TOKYO • MILAN

The state flower depicted on the cover of this book is
Rocky Mountain columbine.

Janet Dailey Americana edition published August 1986
Second printing March 1988
ISBN 373-21906-7

Harlequin Presents edition published December 1976
Second printing June 1979
Third printing February 1982

Original hardcover edition published in 1975
by Mills & Boon Limited

CHAPTER ONE

Outside the sky was a pale blue as if it had been bleached by the searing sun. The trees that lined the street wore thick coverings of rich green leaves. Neighboring lawns with nurtured grass and immaculately trimmed shrubs contrasted sharply with the gleaming oyster shell coloring of pavements and driveways. Behind the gleaming brick and wood homes lived the staid, affluent and cultured society of Denver, Colorado.

Lainie MacLeod stared through the gauze of white sheer curtains, her arms crossed and her hands rubbing her elbows in a gesture of nervousness. A bright yellow dandelion looked back at her from its solitary location on the front lawn. Her hazel eyes noticed the intruder as she sighed wearily. What they really needed, she thought dejectedly, was a part-time gardener, but she knew there was no way to stretch the budget to include him. Somehow she would just have to find time to do it herself, just as she had done with so many other things.

There was really no need to keep up any pretense that the income in this home even came near to equaling that of others on the block. Lainie was sure their neighbors were fully aware of the precarious financial position they were in. No matter how discreet she had tried to be, there was no way they could have missed seeing the consistent removal of priceless objects from the home. Only Lainie's pride refused to allow the outward appearance of the home that she had been reared in to show the true state of their affairs.

A shiny sports convertible turned into their driveway, its driver stopping the car and running her hands through her silky brown hair before hopping out of the car. Lainie smiled as she moved to the front door, glancing up the open staircase toward her mother's bedroom. The last thing she wanted was for the front doorbell to ring and rouse her mother, who had just drifted off to sleep.

It would mean endless explanations as to the reason for Ann Driscoll's visit, and Lainie wasn't ready to explain. Her mother had never approved of her friendship with Ann, insisting that Ann did not exhibit the breeding and culture that had always been expected of Lainie. It was immaterial that Ann's parents were wealthy people, or that Ann had married well. Mrs. Simmons considered Ann's outlook bohemian and treated her as such. But Lainie's own determination had kept their friendship intact.

Lainie knew Ann as the only true friend she had, the only one who had stood by her in any crisis. So when she greeted her at the door, her welcome was genuinely warm. Ann's greeting was just as fervent as always, her emotions mirrored in her eloquent blue eyes which never failed to reflect her feelings whether they be happy, sad, flirtatious or angry. Yet for all her elation at meeting her best friend, Lainie still remained subdued, her eyes straying to the door at the top of the stairs.

As the pair retreated to the kitchen at the rear of the house, Ann's eyes studied Lainie with concern. To a stranger, she would have seemed an enchantingly haunting woman, but to Ann, who had known her for over ten years, the telltale signs of strain were very apparent. The dark circles under her eyes, which heightened the incredibly dark lashes and the almond-shaped hazel green eyes, revealed nights of interrupted sleep. The tan and white checked skirt hung loosely around her waist, and the short-sleeved white linen blouse with its scooped neck accented the prominence of her collarbones. Both indicated the weight loss that was robbing Lainie of her energy. Even her dark hair, which had once been so well cared for that it gleamed with a satiny sheen, was now dull. Now that Lainie had so little time to care for it, she had drawn it away from her face and caught it at the back of her neck with a gold clasp. The severe style further emphasized her always prominent cheekbones, but with an uncomplimentary result.

But Ann also knew that any expression of her concern would be wasted, so she blinked away her anxiety and smiled as she accepted the tall glass of punch offered her.

"How's your mother? Did the doctor stop in this morning?" Ann watched the fleeting frown pass across Lainie's smooth forehead before she replied with deliberate lightness.

"Yes. He seemed very pleased with her, which irritated mother considerably." Lainie sighed heavily as she seated herself at the round table. "She complains so often of the pain that it's difficult to know how serious her condition is at times. And poor Doctor Henderson swears she reads father's medical books just to come up with new symptoms for him to diagnose."

"But everything is all set for tonight?"

"I mentioned it to him." Lainie met the questioning glance, indecision in her own eyes. "He felt as long as there was someone competent staying with mother, it would be all right."

"Who could be more competent than a registered nurse?" Ann shrugged airily.

"I just don't feel right about it." Lainie tapped the edge of her glass nervously. "Mother is so uncomfortable with strangers around. I think it would be best if we postponed it until another time."

"Listen, we've done nothing but talk about this concert for a month now. It's all settled. Adam has bought the tickets and everything. You just can't back out now!"

Little sparks of blue fire flashed out of Ann's

eyes as Lainie hedged at meeting her gaze. She chose instead to lean an elbow on the table and rub her forehead.

"I have been looking forward to the concert," Lainie admitted, "but I just can't help worrying about mother."

"You ought to start worrying about yourself for a change," Ann retorted sharply. "The worst mistake you ever made was coming back here to Denver when your mother became ill. You should have put her in a nursing home instead of knocking your brains out trying to take care of her yourself. In the seven months you've been back, how many times have you been out of this house? And I'm not referring to trips to the pharmacy or grocery store."

"I don't know. A few times," Lainie replied reluctantly.

"I'll tell you exactly. Three times! Once to have dinner with us, once to go shopping with me, and once to the cinema." Ann curtailed her growing anger and leaned forward to plead, "Lainie, if you don't make some time for yourself you're going to have a breakdown."

"Don't be melodramatic!"

"I'm not. You'd just better look in the mirror and discover that you aren't Florence Nightingale. You're not indispensable. Someone else can look after your mother just as adequately as you."

"Oh, Ann!" Lainie's generous mouth curved

into a smile. "If only I could be as sensible as you, perhaps I wouldn't feel so guilty."

"It's your mother who's making you feel guilty. She's running your life just as she's always done. Those three years spent in Colorado Springs have forced her to change her tactics and use emotional blackmail to retie the umbilical cord."

"I had no choice," Lainie replied, her pride stiffening her chin. "There was no money left from father's estate and mother had allowed her insurance to lapse. She may not be the kind of mother that...that I would like her to be, but I would never humiliate her by forcing her to accept someone else's charity."

"And how long will your money last?" Ann asked quietly.

"It doesn't matter." Lainie couldn't bring herself to tell her friend that her money had run out over a month ago and the bills were still coming in. The little income her mother received combined with Lainie's monthly check from Rad were the only things that were keeping food on the table and a roof over their heads.

"All right, it doesn't matter and it's none of my business." Ann's cupid bow lips pursed into a tight line. She leaned over the table toward Lainie, the frustrated urgency she felt visible in her expression. "But you must come to the concert tonight. The chances of Curt Voight returning to Denver in the near future are terribly small. I won't let you miss it if I have to drag you there!"

Voight was a superb pianist, one Lainie had admired for several years. She knew she would be foolish to turn down an opportunity to see him perform in person, especially in the face of Ann's opposition. In the last several years there had been few occasions when she had been able to attend such exclusive events, not since Rad.... There was a sharp, vigorous shake of her head at the unwanted memory.

"I'm going," Lainie said quietly, while Ann wondered what had caused the flicker of pain in the hazel green eyes.

THE NURSE, Mrs. Forsythe, arrived at six that evening so that she would be able to assist Lainie with her mother's dinner and allow Mrs. Simmons an opportunity to adjust to her daughter's absence that evening. Lainie had refrained from informing her earlier because she knew her mother would not be in favor of the idea. And she was absolutely correct.

"Oh, Lainie darling, please don't leave me." Her mother clutched her hand tightly as Lainie seated herself on the bed. Her dainty, superbly feminine features were drawn in petulant lines.

"You're going to be just fine, mother," Lainie soothed her, glancing over at the sympathetically raised eyebrows of the nurse. "Mrs. Forsythe is a very competent nurse. She's been trained to take care of people in your condition."

"But you are my daughter." Her white chin

trembled fretfully. "What if something should happen to me? What if I should die? I want you to be here with me."

"Nothing is going to happen to you," Mrs. Forsythe inserted in a comforting voice. "And with as much spunk as you're displaying, I think it's highly unlikely that you'll die tonight."

Mrs. Simmons immediately reversed her tactics and sunk weakly against her pillow. Her lashes fluttered toward Lainie to show how little strength she had.

"Mrs. Forsythe knows exactly how to get in touch with me. I can be home in minutes if necessary, but either way I promise you I'll come straight home after the concert."

"You won't dally around with that wretched girl, will you?"

"No, mother, I'll come straight home."

Her eyelids closed slowly as if to show Lainie that she was making the supreme sacrifice by allowing her daughter to leave her in the hour of her death. Not even the aging wrinkles on her face could take away the remnants of Mrs. Simmons's youthful beauty, nor her ability to portray the helpless female. Lainie knew this sudden show of emotion was supposed to make her feel guilty at leaving. It succeeded admirably, but it didn't change her mind.

A hand touched her shoulder and Lainie turned.

"Perhaps it would be best if you left her with me," the nurse whispered.

Lainie nodded and retreated quietly from the room. Her mother feigned sleep, but Lainie wasn't deceived. It was merely another ruse that would force Lainie to return to her room before she left for the concert and thus allow Mrs. Simmons another chance to persuade her not to go.

Lainie fought the forces of guilt that assaulted her, refusing to give in to the blackmail her mother was so excellent at providing. The only trouble was that her only weapon was self-pity, which could do little to bolster her already dying desire to attend the concert. This concert had been the only thing she had looked forward to in nearly five years and now she doubted if she'd even enjoy it.

Her lips twisted bitterly at the realization. What a thing for her to admit at twenty-six, she thought. Once she had been the toast of Denver society, the most sought-after girl in the state. And now what was she? A recluse? Forced to care for her mother while the years passed by? How selfish and cynical such thoughts sounded, as if she were totally unmindful of the seriousness of her mother's condition. Yet she did care, Lainie decided sadly. She didn't object to nursing her mother. It wasn't that at all that made her so depressed at times. It was the knowledge that she would never know the happiness of love again.

Once Lainie had blamed her mother for that; now she shouldered the blame herself. It was her own ignorance and inexperience that had persuaded her to listen to her mother, just as she had listened to her in the past. Lainie stared at her reflection in the mirror while brushing her long, thick hair with indifference. She remembered well the summer of her seventeenth year when her mother began "remaking" her. The words drifted back as clearly as if they had been spoken yesterday.

"It's a pity you didn't inherit my looks." Mrs. Simmons studied her daughter with regal indifference. "Beauty is what's going to move you ahead in this world, Lainie. So don't ever be afraid to trade on it, to use it to get what you want."

Lainie had stared at her petite, dainty mother, every short inch of her displaying confidence and dominance.

"I'll never be as beautiful as you," Lainie had sighed wistfully, looking at her own discordant features and tall frame.

"Yes, you will," her mother had replied. "Yours will not be the wholesome beauty of a female, but the striking looks of a woman. First of all, there's your hair—a rich sable brown and your most important asset. You will wear it long," she had ordered, "and we'll pull it out and away from your face. Your cheekbones are much too prominent to hide, so we'll emphasize them...."

So it had gone on, her mother taking each feature and instructing Lainie on the way to show them to the best advantage. Her lips were generous, so they must always be shiny and inviting. The almond shape of her eyes was to be emphasized to make them different from the round, innocent eyes of her friends. The green in her hazel eyes was to be accented to make it more noticeable. Lainie's wardrobe had consisted of only the simplest and most superbly cut dresses, nothing that would detract from her face.

The result was that Lainie was the most arresting, strikingly beautiful girl in her group. She had been popular beyond her wildest dreams, the envy of other girls who could no longer bring themselves to be friends with a girl who provided them with so much competition. All except Ann, who simply admired Lainie's looks and didn't see her as a threat to her own future happiness.

Lainie knew of only two people who had ever liked her for herself. Ann was one. Her fingers trailed over the picture on her dresser as she studied the fun-loving blue eyes that beamed out at her. And her father had been the other, with his smiling eyes and iron gray hair as thick and full as her own. He had been a surgeon of incomparable abilities who had been taken from them in a plane crash nearly two years ago. He had only wanted happiness for her, never desiring to trade on her success as her mother had. He had admired Rad so much and he had been so upset with Lainie when.... She refused again to allow those memories back.

Instead she hurried to the bathroom off her bedroom, forcing her mind to concentrate on the evening at hand. But the past kept returning with incredible persistence. Although Lainie's wardrobe was extensive, all her gowns seemed to be a size too large because of her recent weight loss. She knew of only one dress that would not accent her thinness, and it was pushed to the rear of the closet. Her hands trembled as she withdrew the black lace gown. It had always been Rad's favorite. She had promised herself numerous times that she would give it away or burn it, but it had remained tucked away, out of sight but never out of mind. For one brief moment she almost thrust it back before she chided herself for letting such an association prevent her from wearing the only gown that was becoming to her.

By the time Ann and her husband had picked Lainie up, driven to the concert hall and parked, it was nearly time for the performance to start. It was nearly impossible for Lainie not to remember the times she had been in the hall before. The memories brought the familiar hollow feeling inside as the trio were escorted to their seats. Not until Voight was on stage and had started playing his second piece was Lainie able to push aside her recollections and give herself up to his music.

The intermission came all too quickly. Yet the classically beautiful music had uplifted Lainie's spirits. Her face was more vibrantly alive than Ann had seen it in several years. Her footsteps were eager and her smile generous as she joined Ann and Adam in the exodus to the lobby. Lainie nodded easily when Ann excused herself to phone home to check on her four-year-old daughter, Cherry. The perfection of her contentment was so complete that when a shoulder jostled her roughly, Lainie turned her pardoning expression on the culprit. A blond head tilted toward her inquiringly as a slow smile spread across the handsome face.

"Lainie," he breathed softly. "It *is* you!"

"Lee!" she echoed in the same stunned voice he had used, allowing him to retain her hand in a fiercely gentle grasp. "It's been ages!"

"You're more beautiful than I remembered." His light blue eyes traveled admiringly over her face. "Where have you been hiding? The last time I heard, you were in Colorado Springs."

"I've only been back in Denver a short time." Lainie smiled as she studied the strong, quiet features. She couldn't help wondering how many more of her old crowd were here.

"You've changed. There's a quietness about you that I don't recall. What happened to that sassy little girl?"

"She's grown up, I hope," Lainie laughed as she gently withdrew her hand from his. "Tell me, how is everyone in the old crowd? I read in the paper that MaryBeth was married."

"Most of them have never grown up," Lee Walters answered her first question. "As for Mary-Beth, she's married, but she hasn't changed."

Lainie wasn't really interested in what he was saying. She was busy gathering together her impressions of this attractive man. He hadn't really changed through the years. There was still something about his strong, silent face that lulled you into feeling safe and secure. His smile, slow and sincere, still had the irresistible charm as before. But there was nothing staid and dull about him. Lee had always been capable of being as gay and fun-loving as the rest of their group, yet in a different way.

Since she wasn't listening closely to his words, it wasn't until he raised his hand and motioned to someone behind her that Lainie realized he intended for someone to join them.

"My sister Carrie was just talking about you the other day. She'll be pleased to see you." Lee smiled at her. He started to speak again, but the words died on his lips as he concentrated on the people behind Lainie.

Curiosity at his sudden silence turned her around just as his sister called out gaily, "Look who I've found, Lee!"

Lainie was barely aware of the hush that fell over their small group or of the uncomfortable glances exchanged between Lee, his sister, and her escort. Only the fifth person claimed her attention, the tall, dark-haired man who stared back at her with arrogant coldness as he nonchalantly inhaled on his cigarette. The blood had washed away from her face and was pounding loudly in her ears. Her legs trembled beneath her as she wished hopelessly that the floor would open up and swallow her. No one seemed capable of speech. No one, that was, except the man whose eyes flicked so contemptuously over Lainie.

"The years haven't treated you kindly," he sneered, his gaze picking out the shadows under her haunted eyes and the pallor in her cheeks. "What a pity to be robbed of your beauty so early."

Her face flamed immediately with anger and rage. "You haven't changed, Rad. You're still a ruthless, cold-blooded male swine!"

Dark brown eyes glittered at her ominously as the others inhaled sharply at her sudden attack Lainie ignored them, as did Rad, while sparks continued to fly between their stares. The smoke from his cigarette no longer veiled his face from her and Lainie studied it challengingly. It wasn't a handsome face, because the features looked as if they had been carved with a blunt chisel. The line of his mouth was cruel and the set of his jaw and chin was uncompromising. His expression was unchanging, truly leading one to think it had been carved in stone. Yet the full potence of his masculine virility was visible, making Rad compellingly attractive.

"Your tongue is as sharp as it ever was," he mused. The apathetic tone of his voice made his gibe hurt more, but Lainie didn't have an opportunity to comment. "What are you doing here?"

She drew herself up so that all five foot eight inches of her in heels was standing rigidly in front of him. "I wasn't aware this was a private concert for your benefit only."

There was a certain satisfaction in seeing his nostrils flare in anger at her sarcastic retort. "You know very well I didn't mean that." His voice was threateningly soft.

"My parents—" Lainie halted and corrected herself "—my mother lives here, or had you forgotten?"

"I . . . I heard about your father's death." There was no sympathy in Rad's voice and his mouth twisted cynically. "My father died recently, too."

That was news to Lainie. She had always admired Rad's father. "I'm sorry, I didn't know." Her sincere condolence was impulsive, but he immediately made her regret it.

"There's a bitter touch of irony in knowing the only thing they lived for was to see their grandchildren born." Rad's lips curled scornfully at her. "A desire you didn't want to have happen."

The vicious slur took her breath away and encased her chest in tight, constricting steel bands. "You're an unbelievably cruel man." Lainie couldn't stop her voice from trembling violently.

"Because I wanted a son and you wanted more good times?" Rad sneered.

Lainie turned away, unable to endure any more of his twisting the knife in her heart. Carrie Walters moved toward her, reaching out with her hand to touch Lainie's arm.

"I didn't know you were with Lee," she said softly with the utmost sympathy.

Lainie smiled and nodded, still feeling Rad's censorious eyes on her back. "It's all right," she said after she had found her voice. "My friends will be looking for me. I'd better get back."

"I heard your mother was ill," said Carrie. "I do hope she's better."

"She's doing quite well." Lainie glanced up at the blond-haired man in front of her, his gaze reaching out to silently reassure her. "It was nice seeing you again, Lee."

But before Lainie could excuse herself from them, a hand imprisoned her arm and she was staring again into Rad's cold face.

"Is that why you're back? I heard your father made a lot of bad investments. His estate must have been in shambles. Did you hope to get money from me to take care of your mother?"

The arrogant sarcasm in his face repulsed Lainie. She raised her hand and with all the force she could muster slapped his face. "I'd sell myself in the streets before I'd ask you for anything!"

His rage exploded around her like a volcano and his violent grip made her a part of the upheaval. Fear coursed through her as Lainie realized just how successful she had been at riling him. This was not the first time she had glimpsed this savage side to him, but it was still terrifying.

"MacLeod!" Lee's hand restrained Rad's arm. "MacLeod, let her go."

Lainie watched the clenching of his jaw as Rad slowly regained control of his anger. His chest rose and fell with rapidity even though the dark fires in his eyes slowly returned to their impassive blankness. Slowly he released her arms, stepping back to straighten his tie and adjust the jacket of his black evening suit. Her heart was still beating erratically as Rad moved slowly away from the group. His gaze passed haughtily over each of them, daring them to reproach his actions, before moving with unruffled composure out of sight.

From the corner of her eye Lainie saw Lee turning toward her, his expression plainly that of one about to champion her cause. Her head shook from side to side, seeing the expressions of pity in the eyes of the crowd of spectators. The tears that had been faithfully waiting now sprang into her eyes as she covered her mouth to muffle the choking sobs. Her flight to the powder room went unchecked. The few who might have chosen to follow her were halted by the announcement that the intermission was over and the performance was to begin again. Only the maid saw the full torment of Lainie's pain.

Her mind screamed again the agonizing and bitter words they had exchanged, bringing more wrenching sobs born from her heart. Lainie wasn't even aware of Ann entering the room and cradling her in her arms. Not until the spasms of pain were reduced to choking sobs did Ann attempt to find out what had happened.

"Rad. He's here." Lainie turned her red eyes to the face of her anxious friend. "During the intermission...oh, God...." Fresh sobs broke out while Ann patted her arm comfortingly. "He was so...so frankly cruel. The things we s-said Ann, I...I can't stay here. I've got to go home."

Her fingers clutched Ann tightly. She was ashamed of her childish outburst, but the heartbreaking agony of the last minutes had robbed her of the little pride she had left.

"I'll get a taxi." Lainie straightened up, wiping the tears from her eyes and attempting to get control of her emotions. "There's no need for you and Adam to leave."

"Don't be ridiculous." Ann smiled. "Adam can get the car and will meet us outside in five minutes. The concert wasn't that good anyway."

"Ann...." Lainie sought for words to express her gratitude.

"Sssh! I'll be back."

Ann must have explained the situation to Adam, because when Ann returned to accompany Lainie to the car he shrugged off Lainie's apologies with an understanding glance. And Lainie smiled back at the man with curly fair hair and twinkling blue eyes.

"I don't know what I did to deserve friends like you," Lainie sighed, leaning back exhaustedly in the front seat between Ann and Adam.

"Probably because you married a man like Rad MacLeod," Adam replied, his now stern gaze watching the glaring headlights of the traffic ahead of them.

"I thought after being separated from him for five years that I would have forgotten all the bitterness and misery." Pain dug deep forrows into her forehead. "But we couldn't even greet each other as two civilized human beings."

"I imagine Sondra viewed the whole scene with her usual perverted satisfaction," Ann commented grimly.

"Sondra?" A vivid picture of Rad's titian-haired secretary leaped in focus in her mind's eye. Lainie stiffened, trying to study her friend in the dim interior of the car. "Was... was she there?"

"I saw her in the lobby as I was phoning home." Lainie could tell that Ann didn't relish admitting that Sondra had been at the concert, especially since it was so obvious that Lainie hadn't known it. "I guessed that Rad must have been there and I could only hope you wouldn't see them."

"Poor Rad." Lainie laughed with incredible bitterness. "He deserves her."

A heavy silence weighed uncomfortably on the trio as the full impact of the disastrous evening settled over them. It seemed right to Lainie that they were shuttered in the dark interior of the car with the impersonal world of streetlights and neon signs outside. It was a struggle to emerge from her cocoon of darkness when Adam finally halted the car in front of her house.

"I'm sure Nurse Forsythe wouldn't mind staying overnight," Ann suggested gently, "if...if you don't feel up to staying with your mother."

"No." Lainie knew she would be sleeping anyway. "It won't be necessary."

"Would you like Ann to stay with you tonight?" Adam offered with generosity so characteristic of them both.

"I'd rather be alone." She shook her head sideways and thanked them again for their kindness and understanding before hurrying into the house to let the nurse know they were waiting outside to take her home.

THE SLEEPING DRAFT had performed its task and her mother was sleeping peacefully when Lainie settled in the lounge chair in her mother's bedroom. It wasn't necessary for her to sit with her, but Lainie knew the bed in the adjoining room had looked too lonely to occupy. At least in the chair she wouldn't have to make a pretense of trying to sleep. Lainie gazed up at the ceiling, letting her memory bring back all that she had been trying to forget.

It was six years ago that she had first met Rad MacLeod at an impromptu gathering after a theater play. Rad had arrived at her friend's house to discuss business with her parents. Lainie remembered whirling out of the room wearing a long flowing gown and stopping abruptly as she saw him standing in the entry hall. There had been something breathtaking about the way he had eyed her, his look flattering and sensual. Minutes later she had cornered Andrea, the daughter of the people Rad had come to see, managed to discover exactly who he was and that his firm was constructing a large industrial plant for Andrea's parents in Oklahoma, and had persuaded Andrea to invite him to their gathering.

Still, Lainie had been slightly surprised when he joined them later. It was obvious from the beginning that he didn't fit in with the fun-loving group. He possessed such self-assurance that he seemed to look on their antics with amusement. The ones in the group that Lainie had been dating suddenly appeared as little boys beside this confident specimen of male virility. Lainie had been startled to discover that his eyes were openly mocking her attempts to flirt with him, as if she were playing an immature game.

"I don't care for this particular kind of entertainment," Rad had said, his gaze critically examining her face and figure with embarrassing thoroughness. "I want to be with you and you want to be with me. May I take you home?"

An exhilarating shiver of fear had raced through her as Lainie had briefly considered her sports car parked in the driveway before she had thrown caution to the wind and agreed to accompany him.

There had followed a week of dinner engagements, phone calls, and nightclub dates, and also her first embrace, which shattered Lainie's illusion that she knew how to kiss. Her bones had turned to marshmallows and Rad's fiery touch had roasted her clear through. It was as if she had been stripped of all her morals and she had become his to command. Lainie had known that their lovemaking in the following four weeks had been completely controlled by Rad. Her love for him was completely irrevocable and without boundaries.

When she was apart from him she had been ashamed at the abandonment with which she had responded to him while she raced to be in his arms again. She could never forget that rapturous night when he had finally proposed to her. They were sitting in the car in front of her house, and Lainie was trying to get control of her senses after Rad had firmly set her away from him. She had known the unsatisfactory feeling of not being fulfilled, and her hazel eyes had looked at him pleadingly. As usual he looked completely unmoved, except for that one betraying cord on the side of his neck that she had come to love because it always revealed that he desired her, too.

"You're either going to have to become my wife or my mistress, Lainie." His dark eyes had gleamed at her through the darkness. "I think I would prefer you as the mother of my children."

At the time, it hadn't bothered her that Rad didn't say he loved her, and she had responded with all the enthusiasm and relief that had been bottled up for weeks. Looking back, Lainie knew he had almost appeared amused at her excitement, but she had been too wrapped up in him to notice it.

Her parents' reactions had been divided. Her father had taken one look at the blissfully happy look in her eyes and given his blessing. Although her mother didn't object to the engagement, she did express her doubts.

"Lainie, darling," she had said, exhibiting a vast amount of parental concern, "you've just turned twenty. Rad MacLeod is eleven years older than you. That isn't a great difference, I know, but he's so much more experienced than you."

"Oh, mother, what can that possibly matter?" Lainie had laughed gaily.

"He's a man driven by ambition. He's accustomed to giving orders, to controlling the lives of the people who work for his firm. Dominating others is second nature to him. See how he's already twisting you to fit in with his plans. Whoever heard of a wedding taking place only two weeks after the engagement? It just isn't done."

"Mother, is that what's bothering you?" Lainie had hugged the resisting woman around the shoulders. "I don't care about a large society wedding. All I want is Rad."

"And he knows it," Mrs. Simmons had retorted grimly. "Already you've allowed him to have the upper hand. Soon he'll be dictating who your friends will be. In a matter of months, you'll be pregnant."

"Naturally we both want children." There had

been a shy blush in Lainie's cheeks, induced by the
thought of the coming intimacy between them and
not the discussion of the results.

"I can see that nothing I say means anything to
you. You're too full of your own blind emotions to
listen to reason. Rad MacLeod is a ruthless and
possessive rake who's chosen someone like you to
give himself the respectability he doesn't wish to
earn."

"How can you say that!" Lainie had been ap-
palled by her mother's attack on the man she was
to marry. "He loves me and wants to marry me.
His family is wealthy. Rad is considered a very
good catch."

"As you say, he loves you," her mother had
agreed, but with a dry note of cynicism that had
frightened Lainie. "I won't stand in the way of
your marriage even though I don't approve of
him. But don't let him stand between you and your
friends. Don't let him separate you from the social
life you've known. And before you bring children
into this world, Lainie Simmons, you wait until
you know for sure what kind of man you've married."

As much as she had tried to push her mother's
warnings to the back of her mind, they kept creeping back. When once she would have accepted a
statement from Rad with the faith of her love,
Lainie found herself examining his words, trying
to see if the comments about her friends were sub-
tly derogatory.

The day of the wedding had arrived swiftly, bringing with it all the culmination of her dreams. It was followed by an idyllic fortnight at Rad's cabin in the Rocky Mountains. He had been as tender and gentle and loving as any bride wanted her groom to be. Yet he had managed to fan the sparks of desire that Lainie had possessed into a full, burning fire that only he could fulfill.

Too soon those days of exploring love's enchantment had ended and they returned to Denver, where Lainie discovered how empty the days were when Rad was at his office and she was home alone. She had tried to content herself with taking care of their new home, but with a maid to do the cooking, and a housekeeper to do the cleaning, and a gardener to take care of the lawns and gardens, she had been an ornament, pretty but not very useful. For a time, the evenings with Rad had made up for the loneliness of the days. Lainie gradually drifted back into her friendships with the old group, spending an afternoon shopping with one, or playing tennis with another. Rad hadn't seemed to mind at all.

Of course, it was during that time that Lainie had met Sondra, her husband's beautiful red-haired private secretary. She had known then the first heartbreaking pangs of jealousy toward this woman who spent more hours with her husband than Lainie did. Thus the little arguments had begun.

Looking back, Lainie could see that it was her

own immaturity that had made the first inroads into their marriage. She had begun to resent the demands of his business, to plead with him to spend more time with her, to spend huge sums of money on clothes to entice him to her side; but Rad had only regarded her with amusement, chiding her occasionally to grow up.

Four months after the wedding had come the first business trip, their first separation. Lainie had accompanied Rad to the airport, only to find Sondra already there.

"I have the tickets and our baggage has already been checked." Sondra's green eyes had glittered triumphantly at Lainie for a brief moment.

"Is she going with you?" Lainie had burst out in anger.

She hadn't been prepared for Rad's reaction. With the same lithe swiftness that had already surprised her for a man as tall as Rad, he had gripped her arm and propelled her to a secluded corner. The outraged anger in his face had made her cower inwardly.

"I will not tolerate any more of your childish displays of jealousy in public." The tight hold on his temper was evident by his cold harshness.

"I don't trust her," Lainie had retorted, refusing to allow him to browbeat her.

"I don't believe you trust me."

"Maybe I don't." Her chin had quivered tremulously before she tossed her head back with airy disdain. "I'm sure you'll enjoy the trip. I've no doubt Sondra will see to it. You've told me more than once how competent and indispensable she is. Now I'm beginning to see why!''

She had stalked away, half expecting Rad to come running after her. But he hadn't. That night Lainie had removed his belongings from their bedroom and put them in the guest bedroom.

That had been a mistake, one that she would never have made if she had known her husband better. It had brought a remoteness into Rad when he returned. Even her sincerely meant apology a few days later didn't remove it. The change in their relationship had hurt and confused Lainie. More and more she had sought consolation in the companionship of her old friends, until it was Rad who was returning home from work before Lainie. Yet her mother's words echoed in her ears and Lainie had refused to give up any of her associations.

The winter that year had brought more than snow. It had brought icy indifference into their house each time Rad walked in the door. The terrible arguments were over, but Lainie had discovered a new grief in the coldness that had taken their place. Then had come the evening when they both had been invited to a very important dinner party by one of Lainie's friends. Rad had arrived home only minutes before they were to have left.

"Did you forget we were invited out tonight?" Lainie had demanded as she met him in the foyer.

"Welcome home," Rad had sneered, walking

past her into the den where he poured himself a stiff drink.

"We're supposed to be there in ten minutes."

The way he had regarded her so clinically had irritated Lainie beyond endurance.

"Call them up and tell them we aren't coming." He had turned his back on her.

"I can't do that!"

"I've had a rough day. That damned party isn't all that important."

"No, it's my friends who are giving it, so naturally it isn't important to you," Lainie had retorted sarcastically.

"Your constant bitching is getting on my nerves." Rad's jaw had been tightly clenched and Lainie had blanched in spite of her air of defiance. "I am not going to that party tonight, and that's final!"

"Well, I am!"

"I'd think about it if I were you," Rad had said coldly as Lainie had turned to leave the room.

"Is that some kind of threat?" She had spun around sharply.

"I think it's time you made a choice between your husband and your friends."

"Is that your solution to saving our marriage?" Her mother's warnings had come echoing back in that moment. "Or do you think the patter of little feet would more effectively tie me down?"

"I would have been better off taking you as my mistress instead of my wife."

The complete lack of emotion in Rad's voice had taken Lainie's breath away. There had been no further doubt in her mind that what love he had felt for her was gone. She had left the room, shaky legs carrying her farther away from him.

CHAPTER TWO

ANN DROPPED IN the following afternoon. The concern that had haunted her from last night had proved to be warranted once she had looked at Lainie's sleepless face.

"You should have let me stay with you last night," she scolded grimly.

"We would have talked half the night anyway," Lainie smiled faintly, "and I still wouldn't have had enough sleep."

"Instead you relived the nightmare again." Ann studied her astutely. "You still haven't forgotten him, have you?"

"I loved him once very deeply," Lainie replied quietly. "You can't block out the happy memories altogether."

"Now that you've seen him again, you don't still love him, do you?"

"No." It was a breathy protest with a tiny gleam of uncertainty in Lainie's eyes. Last night Rad had taken her by surprise. That was why her heart had beat so wildly.

"Was there never any talk of you two getting together again? When you first broke up, I mean?"

Ann asked. "You told me that Rad refused to give you a divorce."

"When we were first married, I loved him so much I let my heart rule my head." Lainie turned her unseeing gaze to the gold flocked paper on her bedroom wall. "I was jealous of every minute he spent away from me. I resented his work, his associates, anything that deprived me of him. I behaved like a child, spending money to draw attention to myself, deliberately going to parties without him, trying to make him jealous. I often wonder if I'd been more mature and understanding if we wouldn't still be married today. If I wouldn't still be blissfully ignorant of what a hollow shell our marriage was from the beginning."

"What are you talking about?" Never in the few times that Lainie had discussed her marriage with Ann had she ever made such a statement.

Lainie stared down at her long slim fingers, interlocking her hands. "Rad never loved me." A shimmering veil of tears covered the hazel green eyes as she met Ann's startled glance with quiet dignity. "He told me so. Physically I was desirable and socially I was acceptable, so I was the prime candidate when he decided to take a wife."

"Of all the cold-blooded—" Ann exploded briefly, before turning puzzled eyes on Lainie. "Then why didn't he give you a divorce?"

"I believe he said he had paid dearly to marry me and he wasn't going to pay to get rid of me."

She tried to make her voice light and uncaring, but the pain of that memory went too deep. "I began shouting at him, telling him I didn't want his money, that I just wanted to be free of him, and if he didn't give me a divorce, I'd sue him for one." Lainie twisted her head to the side as she remembered the final humiliation Rad had placed on her. She bit her lip to keep control of its quivering while Ann waited silently for her to continue. "He called in one of his engineers, had him come to the room where we were. I can still remember the cold, calculating tone of Rad's voice as he asked the man whether he had ever had any. . . any relationship with me while I was married to Rad. The man said that he had, several times."

Ann drew a sharp breath.

"Rad laughed after the man left and told me that was the only kind of divorce that I would ever get. He said he could get all kinds of men who would testify to the same thing. He suggested that I be content with a separation, since that was all he was prepared to offer me."

"Why didn't you ever tell me this before, Lainie? It explains so many things I never understood before." Ann smiled compassionately at her friend. "When you two first split up, I was astonished by the change in you. You seemed to lose all confidence in yourself, I thought you were headed for a breakdown."

"If it hadn't been for dad, I probably would

have,'' Lainie admitted. "I remember one evening
he came into my room and found me crying. He
took me in his arms as if I were still a child and
began wiping away my tears. For all his quietness,
dad was a very philosophical man. I'll never forget
what he told me. 'The rainbow comes after the
storm, so first you must endure the storm.' '' She
glanced briefly at Ann. "That's why I left Denver,
to start my life over and wait for the storm to pass.
I thought it had.''

"Until you saw Rad again.''

"Yes. Last night I was tossed right back into the
heart of it.''

The tinkling of a bell filtered into the room,
followed by a very plaintive call from the occupant
of the adjoining room.

"I thought your mother was sleeping,'' Ann
whispered as Lainie jumped to her feet.

"She was.'' Lainie's forehead was knitted in a
frown. She motioned for Ann to remain where she
was as she walked swiftly to the connecting door,
which she had left partially ajar.

Dainty pink and rose-colored flowers spread
their gay pattern around with complementing pink
satin curtains at the windows, complete with ruf-
fles. The elegant marble-topped dressing table at
the far side of the room was hidden by delicate
Dresden figurines and fragile glass ornaments.
From the pink-canopied bed came Mrs. Simmons's repeated summons for Lainie. Her light

gray hair matched the pastel room, as did her pale complexion.

"What is it, mother?" Lainie patted the slender hand that reached out for her.

"I heard you talking in the other room." Round blue eyes fluttered questioningly at Lainie. "You were talking about Rad. Lainie, you aren't seeing him again, are you?"

"No, of course not. I merely ran into him at the concert last night," Lainie assured her.

"You didn't...you didn't tell him about our difficulties! You didn't mention how poor we've become?" The plaintive cry of pride in her mother's voice tugged at Lainie's heart. "I couldn't bear it if he knew."

Lainie nibbled at her lower lip before smiling with determined assurance. "I didn't ask him for a thing, mother," she answered truthfully.

"Good," Mrs. Simmons sighed, and her hand moved weakly away from Lainie's to rest on the pink satin quilt across her breast. "I can rest now."

It was a dismissal, with all the affected regal air that was common to her mother. Lainie often wondered how much of her mother's weakness was an act and how much was real. It was so difficult to tell, but her illness was genuine.

TWO DAYS LATER Lainie finally found time to do the weeding of the front lawn. Her mother had taken her sedative an hour before and had fallen asleep immediately. It was rather a blessing being out in the sunlight, feeling its warmth penetrating her light cotton blouse and cream-colored slacks. Summer was nearing its end. Lainie knew these days of sunshine would soon be blotted out by the cold blast of winter's breath sweeping down out of the Rocky Mountains.

The perspiration on her forehead trickled down her face, but the physical exertion was relaxing. The digging and tugging to remove the stubborn weeds demanded concentration. Her mind had been working overtime these last few days, worrying over their financial woes while fighting off the persistent memories of Rad. Lainie had been sure that she had driven him from her thoughts, but after their explosive meeting the other night she found all the bitterness and misery had returned.

Firm steps sounded behind her, swishing through the grass. Lainie turned slightly from her kneeling position, shading her eyes from the sun's glare to identify the person approaching her.

"Well, Lee, what a surprise!" She rose to her feet, removed the cotton glove from her hand and extended it warmly to him.

"I didn't know gardeners came in such attractive models." Lee smiled, his blue eyes lighting up at the pleased expression on Lainie's face.

"Won't you come up to the house?" She flushed under the intensity of his gaze. "I'm afraid I'm not really dressed for company. It'll only take me a minute to freshen up."

"You look beautiful. There's a glow to your cheeks that's especially becoming." He turned her toward the house and firmly tucked her hand through his arm. "I haven't been able to get you out of my mind, so I decided to stop."

"Flatterer!" Lainie laughed, glancing up at the strong face beneath the blond brown hair.

"No, it's not flattery," Lee replied. The sincerity in his eyes caused Lainie to falter a little. "I haven't been able to get you out of my mind for several years. Before, I waited too long to let you know how I felt about you. This time, now that I've found you again, I'm going to plunge in first before anyone else has a chance."

"You don't give a girl an opportunity to think." Lainie's footsteps had halted as she stared in astonishment at Lee.

"Neither did Rad McLeod," Lee replied quietly, watching the blood flow away from Lainie's face. "And you married him."

"I'm not as impetuous as I once was. I won't make the same mistake again." She firmly withdrew her hand from his.

"I'm glad." He smiled that quiet, serene smile that always produced a feeling of security in Lainie. "Because I would want you to be very sure of yourself before you married me."

"You're going too fast!" She shook her head as if to free herself from the web that was being spun around her. "We haven't seen each other for five years. You can't begin to know me, nor I you."

"Then I suggest we get acquainted again. Have dinner with me this evening?"

"Lee, my mother is bedridden. She can't be left alone. It's out of the question for me to consider dating anyone," Lainie explained, lifting her chin proudly as she met his steady gaze.

"Would you object if I called on you here in your home? Because I won't be put off."

"What can I say?" Her shoulders lifted in bewilderment. "We've known each other a long time. I've always considered you as a friend, and now all of a sudden you're trying to change that. You're confusing me."

"As a friend, may I come over some evenings, then?"

"My friends are always welcome," Lainie replied.

"How about offering this friend something cold to drink?"

As quickly as Lee had become serious, he became lighthearted and gay. He had followed Lainie unperturbed into the kitchen and had relaxed at the table, discussing nothing more serious than the whereabouts of various acquaintances they had in common. Lainie was left with the feeling that the previous conversation had never taken place. Except that she knew it had. An uneasiness gripped her, which made it difficult for her to react naturally to the situation.

She found herself examining her own feelings. After her disastrous marriage to Rad, she didn't know if she wanted to become involved with anyone else to that extent again. But there was no doubt that Lee was pleasing company, nor that he was a dependable person. Then the whole situation struck her as being humorlessly academic anyway and she mocked herself for being so concerned about it. After all, she was still legally married to Rad.

Now that Lee had declared his intentions, the most sensible thing for her to do was to sit back and wait to see what happened. Although she had been loath to admit it to herself before, Lainie had been lonely with only her invalid mother for company and an occasional visit from Ann. As long as Lee maintained this lighthearted attitude, what was the harm in letting him visit her a couple of times a week?

The following evening Ann phoned her and Lainie mentioned Lee's visit and his intention to come over that Friday. She wasn't exactly attempting to get Ann's advice, but she was curious to see what her friend's reaction would be to the situation. Ann endorsed it.

"Lee is exactly what you need," she said firmly. "Someone who's solid and dependable who won't be bouncing you around as if you were on the end of a yo-yo."

"You make him sound like an old shoe!" Lainie chuckled. "I don't think he'd appreciate that. He's really quite a handsome man, always has been."

"Yes, but there's that air of security about him, which is exactly what you need right now." There was a great deal of grim determination in Ann's voice. It startled Lainie.

"Why do you say that?"

"It's just a feeling I have." Lainie could almost visualize Ann shrugging her shoulders as she said that. "What I really called for was to invite you to lunch with me tomorrow. My mother came over today and mentioned she'd been wanting to call on your mother but she wasn't sure whether she should or not. So I volunteered her to visit tomorrow noon."

"I'd love to go—"

"No 'buts,' please. My mother was a nurse a long time ago," Ann inserted. "She isn't likely to panic if your mother should take a bad turn. Besides, with my mother there to talk her ear off, she won't even miss you."

"I do have a prescription for her that needs to be filled," Lainie admitted hesitantly. "I suppose I could do that while I'm out."

"There, you see. If you really want to find an excuse, there's always one available." Ann laughed. "We'll be over tomorrow about eleven-thirty."

"I'LL HAVE the chef's salad," Lainie ordered, glancing over the menu briefly before smiling up at the waiter, "with the house's blue cheese dressing. Coffee later."

As Lainie had expected, Ann had brought her to one of the more plush restaurants in town. Elegant chandeliers hung in clusters from the ceilings with all the abundance of evergreen garlands at Christmas time. The muted voices of the room's occupants mingled with the tinkling of crystal and the ring of silver. White linen tablecloths stretched over the endless reaches of tables graced by chairs covered wtih gold velvet. Lainie draped her napkin over the gentle olive shade of her skirt, unbuttoning the matching jacket to reveal the ivory shell beneath.

"Do you suppose they're still discussing your mother's illness, or have they progressed to our childhood maladies?" Ann grinned at her conspiratorially after the waiter had left.

"My mother has many symptoms. They should be through about half of them," Lainie replied, her eyes twinkling with amusement while she took a sip of the ice-laden water in her goblet. "How is it that Adam didn't snap you up for lunch today?"

"There was some directors' meeting of his firm this morning and he was sure it would carry over through lunch. So I polished his briefcase this morning and made sure he wasn't wearing trousers with a shiny seat before sending my young executive husband off to the lion's den." Then Ann's mercurial manner changed abruptly from suppressed giggles to intense interest. "Now, you tell me more about Lee."

Lainie recounted again Lee's visit of yesterday

and suffered through Ann's matchmaking tendencies with ready wit. It always seemed that when her sense of humor had vanished, Ann would pop over and tease it to the surface again. There were times when her friend refused to take any situation seriously and Lainie was given no choice but to do the same. Yet laughter kept all her other woes in their proper place. With Ann around, they never had the opportunity to take control.

The time passed swiftly. No sooner, it seemed, had they sat down at the table than their meal was finished and they were lingering over their coffee. Ann made another audaciously funny comment about Lee's prospects as a future lover and sent Lainie into peals of laughter.

"You make me feel like a schoolgirl again." Lainie brushed her long hair away from her face, her lips still twitching with laughter. "Giggling over my latest conquest."

"That's the idea," Ann retorted brightly. As her gaze strayed over Lainie's shoulder her eyes suddenly glinted with the fire of battle. "Damn," she whispered, "why does he have to be here?"

Lainie glanced over her shoulder, her own hazel eyes still sparkling with humor, to see who had drawn such an angry reaction from Ann. She found herself staring into Rad's dark eyes. The muscles in her stomach contracted sharply as she swallowed her laughter. There was a mesmerizing quality about his gaze that held her own even when she wanted to look away. If it hadn't been for the sardonic lines on his face, Lainie could have believed there was a glint of pleasure in his eyes. But that was ridiculous. Rad couldn't possibly be pleased to see her. He was nearly even with their table before Lainie noticed the rest of the people in his party, especially the red-haired girl preceding him who didn't attempt to hide the hostility in her green eyes.

"Mrs. MacLeod!" Sondra exclaimed with a tinge of sarcasm in her husky voice. "What a surprise to see you again!"

"Yes, isn't it?" Lainie could barely stop herself from bristling with old jealousy, but she felt its tremblings as she watched Rad's hand, the one wearing the elaborately scrolled gold wedding band she had given him, touch Sondra's arm.

"Why don't you go on over to our table and tell Bob and Harry I'll be there shortly," Rad suggested to Sondra. The private look that passed between them set Lainie's teeth on edge. After Sondra had departed, accompanied by two other men in business suits, Lainie felt Rad's eyes return to her, causing a tide of warmth to flood through her.

"Was there something you wanted to speak to me about?" She struggled to remain calm, fingering the stem of her water goblet to give her nervous hands something to do.

"I thought there was something you wanted to talk to me about." His mocking tone unwillingly lifted her gaze to where he stood towering above her. "After five years, I've now seen you twice in one week."

"You should mark it in your calendar," Lainie retorted bitterly, "and hope we can make it another five years."

"I doubt if another five years would neutralize your acid tongue." The harsh lines around his mouth and nose twisted with cynicism. "There always was a chemical reaction between us."

"I've already told you there's nothing I want from you," Lainie hissed, "so why don't you just leave me alone!"

Her insides were being twisted into knots. She didn't know how much more she could take without revealing the torment Rad was putting her through. She could hardly look at his perfectly tailored gray suit without remembering the broad tanned chest concealed beneath it, nor look at his dark hair without recalling its softness when she had run her fingers through it.

"Check, please," Ann signaled the waiter with barely disguised impatience.

"Don't let me run you off," Rad jeered. "I'd hate to think I spoiled your luncheon."

"I just bet you wouldn't," Ann retorted, placing her neatly folded napkin on the table and bestowing the full force of her smoldering eyes on Rad.

"It's time I was getting back to mother," Lainie said, knowing quite well that her friend wasn't the kind to hold back her temper. The last thing Lainie wanted was an embarrassing scene in the restaurant.

"Your mother must be feeling better, since her dutiful daughter has left her side to enjoy a casual lunch." Rad didn't spare the sarcasm in his voice or the contemptuous gleam in his gaze.

"Yes, she is better." Lainie breathed in deeply to keep from answering in kind.

"That's an outright lie!" Ann rose from her chair in rigid anger. She spared Lainie a brief apologetic glance before turning on Rad with a vengeance. "Her mother is ill, terminally ill. There's no hope at all that she'll ever recover. And I despise your condescending attitude toward Lainie and her presence at her mother's side at a time like this! Lainie isn't like you. She wouldn't shirk her duties. She gave up her job and everything else to come back here to try to make her mother's last days more comfortable. I will not stand for you abusing her this way! Surely she has enough worries with hospital bills and nursing and all the regular household chores, without you coming back into her life to upset it again!"

"How touching to spring to Lainie's defense." Rad was completely unmoved by Ann's outburst, as he turned his sardonic face toward Lainie. "How did you manage to inspire such loyalty?"

"It must be a recently acquired ability. I never had it when I was with you, did I, Rad?" Lainie answered with cold quietness.

"If I was ever unfaithful, and you don't know

one way or the other, it could have only been because my home life was unsatisfactory. Are you now saying that the question of my fidelity is the cause of our separation?'' His eyebrow lifted arrogantly over his right eye as Rad regarded her with amusement. ''After five years, you can surely come up with something more original than that?''

''Five years, six months and fourteen days ago,'' Lainie corrected in frustration and could have immediately bitten her tongue off at his accompanying laughter.

''You've kept track!'' Rad's triumphant expression was a further irritant.

''People always remember the amount of time they've been free of oppressive tyrants!'' she flashed, and was rewarded by the hardening of his jaw.

''I'm glad you have pleasant memories of something.'' Anger bit through every word as Rad nodded abruptly toward Ann, then back at Lainie. ''I won't keep you any longer. It's obvious you're anxious to be gone.''

Laine watched him striding away with a mixture of relief and sorrow. Their bitterly harsh arguments had always left her weak, and this time had been no different. And, as before, she knew a desire to run after the retreating broad shoulders, to touch his arm and have him stop so that her eyes and lips could beg her forgiveness and feel once again the fire of his caress. But the time when she could do that had passed. So instead she rose to her feet and joined Ann.

"Well, that really blew our relaxing luncheon," Ann sighed. "You aren't going to want to come out with me anymore if he keeps turning up like a bad penny."

"There was no way either of us could know he'd be here." Lainie hid the surge of longing she felt. "Besides, I've run away from him long enough and I'm too tired to try again."

"Do you still love him?" Ann's voice was filled with quiet compassion.

Lainie breathed in deeply to form the words of denial, but as she met her friend's open gaze she sighed, "I'm not sure. I'm not sure about anything."

"Rad is a hard man to forget." Ann stared in the direction Rad had taken.

Lainie silently agreed with her, fervently praying that someday she would be able to forget him and the emotion she had once felt for him.

THE NEXT DAY, knowing that Lee would be coming over that night, Lainie responded to the demands of the house to clean its nooks and crannies. She tried to convince herself that it was because of Lee and not any desire to fill her time with work instead of thoughts of Rad MacLeod. Unfortunately her mother was excessively restless, constantly ringing the little silver bell at her bedside for her, making progress in the housework difficult and nearly impossible. Lainie had lost count of the number of times that she had laid a duster down or turned the vacuum cleaner off to race up the stairs to her mother. It was already the middle of the afternoon and she hadn't completed the downstairs yet. At this rate, she thought grimly, she would be lucky to have time to shower and change before Lee arrived.

A bell jingled demandingly for her. She was halfway up the stairs before she realized it was the telephone and not her mother that was ringing. With a disgusted sigh she turned around and hurried toward the den.

"Simmons residence," she answered.

"Mrs. MacLeod, please," a male voice replied.

"This is she." An apprehensive chill raced through her as Lainie tried to place the voice and failed.

"Mrs. MacLeod, this is Greg Thomas. I'm a lawyer representing your husband."

Lainie breathed in deeply. Was Rad filing for a divorce? The idea filled her with a feeling of dread.

"Mr. MacLeod would like me to get together with you so that you and I could discuss some changes he would like to make."

"What kind of changes, Mr. Thomas?" Lainie asked quietly. The black telephone receiver in her hand seemed to be made of lead. She had difficulty keeping it to her ear.

"Regarding the token payments you're receiving from your husband each month."

A sickening nausea attacked Lainie's stomach. She knew she had been unforgivably rude to Rad, flashing out with spiteful, bitter statements. But she never dreamed she had angered him to the point where he would withdraw the small sum he had been sending her each month. That tiny check was insignificant by itself, but when coupled with her mother's pension, it enabled them to live.

"My mother is quite ill right now. It's nearly impossible for me to get away." Her voice trembled in spite of her attempt to sound calm and controlled.

"Yes, Mr. MacLeod explained that to me. I believe it was your mother's illness that prompted him to increase your allotment." There was a condescending ring to the lawyer's voice.

"Increase?" Lainie echoed weakly.

"Yes, your husband is aware that your financial circumstances have deteriorated since your separation, and that you must be having difficulties making ends meet now that you're forced to care for your mother. I think it's a very magnanimous gesture on his part."

Mr. Thomas named a figure so much larger than the pittance she received now that Lainie was stunned. She had been expecting the opposite, bracing herself to fight for the little she did receive. The lawyer was speaking again. Lainie had to mentally shake her head to concentrate on what he was saying.

"...illness, you'll have doctor's bills and hospital bills, as well as other expenditures such as medication. No doubt these have piled up on you. Mr. MacLeod has suggested that this increase be retroactive, which would give you a tidy sum to take care of some of your larger debts."

"Why is he doing this?"

"I've just explained, Mrs. MacLeod," the man replied patiently. "He's learned of your mother's illness and is aware of the strain it must have placed on your resources. He certainly didn't mention any other motive. It's a charitable gesture on his part. Now if we could just make an appointment for you to come into my office, there are a few papers for you to sign."

"Charitable." The word struck a sour note.

"That's impossible." Lainie's voice rang out sharply into the receiver, emboldened by the swelling of indignant pride in her chest.

"But, Mrs. MacLeod, I'm sure you would like to have this increase initiated as soon as possible."

"Our previous arrangement was quite adequate," she retorted. "This sudden attack of conscience on my husband's part would be quite touching if it weren't so insufferably arrogant."

"Mrs. MacLeod!" The obvious dismay in the lawyer's voice filled her with amused satisfaction.

"I've managed for five years without the benefit of his pity or charity, if that's what you prefer to

call it. And if my straitened circumstances cause
him too much humiliation, then perhaps he should
get a divorce and thus alleviate any misguided feeling of responsibility for me." She made sure her
words were laced liberally with sarcasm. "You
pass that message on to Mr. MacLeod."

She replaced the receiver with all the finality of a
person cutting her own throat. Heaven knew, she
needed the money.

CHAPTER THREE

"WHO WAS THAT on the telephone this afternoon?" her mother inquired as Lainie walked into the room carrying her dinner tray.

"This afternoon?" Lainie stalled. "Oh, just someone soliciting for magazine subscriptions."

"Are you sure?" Blue eyes blinked appealing up at her. "It wasn't some bill collector and you're trying to shield me from it?"

"Oh, mother, of course not." Lainie smiled widely. For one precarious moment she had been afraid that her mother, with her all-knowing perceptive instincts, knew the nature of the call. "We may be in a rather unsavory position moneywise, but our creditors certainly haven't got to the stage where they're ringing us at all hours and camping on our doorsteps."

"How can you treat it so lightly?" Mrs. Simmons queried, her fingers fumbling with the coverlet in agitation.

"Because you're being so melodramatic about it." Lainie was determinedly light and teasing, having discovered that was the only way she could avoid the tear-jerking sessions where her mother bemoaned for hours the fate that had deprived them of the life-style they had once known. "Now, I've fixed you some delicious broth and a salad. You stop worrying about the bills and eat."

She shook the Irish linen napkin free and placed it over her mother's lap before adding an extra pillow behind her back.

"I really don't feel much like eating. The pain is so much worse today," her mother moaned fretfully.

"You eat as much as you can," Lainie soothed. "I have to shower and change, but I'll be back shortly to see how you've done."

"Is someone coming over?"

"Lee Walters is coming over for a little while this evening."

"We can't really afford to entertain, can we?"

"Will you stop worrying about money!" Lainie raised her eyebrows significantly before leaning over to place a light kiss on her mother's cheek. "I've got a very inexpensive fondue all ready for a light snack."

"Lee Walters," her mother mused softly, her mind already sidetracking itself. "Isn't he the son of Damian Walters?"

"Yes."

"With fair hair and blue eyes. I remember him now. I always thought he was fond of you." Mrs. Simmons smiled wistfully up at her daughter. "But I never encouraged him to come around. His father is filthy rich, but he has this peculiar idea

that his children should make it on their own. I
believe his son is even working as a salesman in his
real estate firm, isn't he?"

"I really don't know, mother."

"You'd think he would at least have given him
an administrative position. I remember Mrs. Walters telling me that all their children received was a
paltry allowance and a car and they had to live on
what they made. Why, their children don't even
have a trust fund set up for them! I wouldn't be
surprised if Damian Walters left all his money to
some charity when he dies." Mrs. Simmons leaned
her head back onto her pillow as if the brief spate
of indignation had weakened her. "Which was the
very reason I wasn't too anxious for you to become involved with his son, even though his family
is very prominent. But considering our present
position, it doesn't really matter anymore. I'm
almost grateful that this boy is coming to call on
you. It makes me feel we're not really social out-
casts."

"I'm glad you don't mind him coming over."
Lainie squeezed her mother's hand. "It's time I
was getting ready. You can do me another favor by
cleaning up your dinner while I'm changing."

"I will."

Lainie blew the fragile figure a kiss as she
walked through the door adjoining her own bedroom. Money, she thought angrily; why did every
conversation always seem to revolve around
money? Or was she just being sensitive because of

the phone call this afternoon, which could have ended many of their problems if only she hadn't allowed her stubborn pride to intervene? She adjusted the water temperature before turning the shower on full force in her ornate black and gold bathroom. In minutes she was undressed and standing under the needle-sharp spray of water, turning so that it could pelt every inch of her and drive out this angry depression that held her.

With the taps turned off, Lainie stepped out of the shower stall and swaddled herself in the large white terry towel, slipping her feet into white mules. Feeling somewhat refreshed, her skin tingling from the force of the pellets of water, Lainie stopped in front of the mirror. She pushed a stray lock of her hair back with the rest piled on top of her head, secured with an oversized pin, before reaching for the jar of moisturizing cream for her face.

The doorbell sounded downstairs, causing Lainie to glance sharply at her gold watch lying on the dressing table. It was too early for it to be Lee, unless he had decided to come sooner. Impatiently she stepped into her culotte-styled lounging robe, the spring green, dotted Swiss fabric enhancing the whiteness of her complexion. She was starting to let her hair down when the bell sounded again.

If only he had given her another quarter of an hour before arriving, she thought uselessly as she sped from her room and down the open staircase, she could have been all ready. The words were already forming in her mind to excuse herself a few more minutes as she flung open the front door.

Her mouth remained open, but no words came out as she stared into the granite-hard face of Rad. The unmistakable fire of challenge in his eyes caused her to step aside, allowing him entry into her home.

"Surely you aren't surprised to see me," he drawled, his eyes raking the thin fabric of her gown with sardonic amusement. "Mr. Thomas passed on your message."

Lainie's hand reached up to clutch the high neckline tighter together, knowing full well that the material was clinging to her still damp skin and emphasizing her curves thoroughly. She turned away as if giving in to the desire to flee from him before pivoting back to face him. She did glance hesitantly up the stairs toward her mother's door.

"If you received my message, then I don't see why you're here." Lainie kept her voice low, not wishing her mother to overhear their voices and recognize Rad's. "I thought I made myself clear. There isn't anything more to discuss."

"That's where you're wrong." His sharply clipped statement revealed the tight hold he had on his temper.

Lainie swallowed convulsively as her eyes roamed nervously over his impeccably tailored blue suit and the gleaming white shirt that contrasted sharply with the golden tan of his skin. Rad still could make her feel vulnerable and inadequate. There was that air of authority about him that always made her arguments seem so futile.

"Then say whatever it is that you've come to say and leave." But her words were choked, betraying his ability to disturb her.

"Here?" Rad's eyebrow lifted in questioning mockery. "Wouldn't it be better to go into the living room where our voices wouldn't carry so easily upstairs?"

"Not the living room," Lainie rushed in, "the . . . the den would be better."

"I prefer the living room." Rad glided past her before she could think of a sound excuse to prevent him.

She stopped just inside the doorway, watching him as he glanced around the room. At first glance the room was elegantly Victorian, with ornate rose-covered chairs and matching sofa, but the discerning eye could pick up the rectangular patches on the wall where the paint was brighter than the rest. Lainie lifted her chin with defiant pride as Rad turned toward her.

"I seem to recall some Impressionist paintings on that wall." To anyone else, Rad's comment would have sounded idly curious, but Lainie knew better.

"We're having them rehung."

"And the sculpture by Robbins that was on the mantel?"

"It's been packed away. We got tired of it."

"I see." Mockery curled the corner of his

mouth. "Did you get tired of that vase your mother was so proud of, the one your father gave her?" Then he smiled smugly. "I suppose it got broken."

"Yes," Lainie retorted sharply.

"It would be interesting to take an inventory and find out how many valuable objects have either been packed away, are being rehung, or were broken." His eyelids lowered lazily to conceal the brilliant fire in his gaze as he studied her with unbearable penetration. "I suppose the jewelry was the first to be sold, wasn't it?"

High color filled her cheeks as she wrapped her arms around herself and turned away from him. "Yes," she hissed, "yes, it was the first."

"Do you know how much you owe? Have you any idea how deeply in debt you are?" Rad stepped closer to her, cold anger filling his face.

She attempted to shrug his question aside, but he wouldn't allow her. He enumerated every creditor and the amount they were due with frightening correctness. Tears burned the back of her eyes, making them incredibly bright when she turned them on him.

"Did it give you pleasure rooting out all our debts?" Her temper flared readily to her lips even though her chin trembled in humiliation. "Did it make you feel superior to discover how poor we've become?"

"Damn you, Lainie! I'm trying to make things easier for you!" Rad's voice was raised to match hers.

"How?" she demanded regarding him sarcastically. "By thrusting your unwanted charity on us? By shaming us more?"

"What do you expect me to do?" He glared at her, exasperated lines carved in his face. "Should I wait until you're eventually forced into bankruptcy? Until your mother and you are bundled into the streets? Am I supposed to treat you like common strangers and be completely unmoved by your plight?"

"How very noble you are!" Lainie spat out at him. "Does it amuse you to become our benefactor? What am I supposed to do to repay you?"

"Nothing! I don't expect any repayment from you," Rad growled through tightly clenched teeth. "You need the money and I'm prepared to see that you get it. It's as simple and uncomplicated as that!"

"With you, nothing is simple and uncomplicated." Her hands were doubled into fists held rigidly at her side. "I won't deny that we need the money, but I won't take a cent of your money. Do you hear me! I don't want your money!"

"You want me to stand by and see you humiliated and embarrassed in front of all your friends, to watch you lose your pride and self-respect, is that it?" He studied her contemptuously.

"Are you afraid they'll blame you?" Lainie challenged. "Do you think they'll condemn you for not stepping forward to help me? Well, don't worry. I'll be sure to tell them of your generosity."

"You crazy little bitch!" Rad grasped her shoulders and shook her hard, dislodging the tears that had remained precariously on the brim of her eyes. "Do you think I care what people say? It doesn't matter to me. It's you I'm worried about."

The pin holding her hair on top of her head unsnapped, sending her dark curls cascading around her face in abundant disarray. The shaking stopped, but her shoulders remained in his grip while her hands rested on the muscular hardness of his chest. A stillness permeated the air between them as Rad studied the tears trickling down her cheeks. Her lips were parted to protest, but Lainie found it impossible to speak. The harshness of his gaze silenced her while inside her senses were vibrating from his closeness.

"Why, Lainie?" his husky voice asked. "You've taken my name. You've taken me into your bed. Why can't you take my money?"

"Rad, please let me go," she whispered. Her almond-shaped eyes pleaded with him to release her.

She watched the scowl lift from his forehead and the look in his eyes change from demand to mockery. And her frightened heart took off at a frantic pace. There was a slight negative movement of his head before he brutally drew her closer to him. One hand gripped the back of her neck with painful fierceness while the other hand slid to the small of her back and forced her body to mold to the hardness of his. Lainie struggled ineffectually against him, but succeeded only in drawing his laughter.

"You want me to," Rad jeered. "It's there in your eyes. It was always like this between us. We fought as violently as we made love."

"No!" Her protest was a breathless murmur even as her pulse leaped in anticipation of his kiss.

Rad didn't disappoint her. His mouth descended on hers with cruel authority, bruising, commanding, possessing, until he at last evoked the response from her that he had been seeking. When his hands firmly moved her away from him, it took only one glance at the satisfied glint in his eyes for Lainie to bow her head in humiliation, her heart aching that she hadn't had the strength to resist him.

"There hasn't been anyone else since me, has there?" Rad's rhetorical question brought her chin up so her eyes, glittering with shame and hurt, could gaze accusingly at him.

Lainie had no ready retort on her lips and no lie came to her mind. But the need to reply was saved by the tinkling of her mother's bell. Rad made no effort to hold her as she moved away on quivering legs. Yet she heard his light footsteps behind her as she made her way into the foyer and to the staircase. She paused once halfway up the steps to glance down at him. His enigmatic dark eyes stared back and Lainie raced the rest of the way to the top.

"Did you want something, mother?" Lainie left the door open as she entered the bedroom.

"Was that the Walters boy at the door? I thought perhaps he could come talk to me. Lainie, you're not dressed!" Her voice rang out with amazing clarity.

"I will be shortly." Lainie had difficulty smiling and her hands shook as she removed the tray of dishes from her mother's bed. "Lee hasn't arrived yet, but when he does, I'll see if he can come up for a few minutes."

She didn't want to prolong the conversation and moved swiftly toward the door.

"Then who rang the doorbell?"

Lainie paused in the doorway to glance down to the bottom of the stairs where Rad stood casually studying the cigarette in his hand, but hearing every word.

"Just a salesman," she answered harshly. "I'm having trouble getting rid of him."

"Well, just tell him you don't want anything."

"I'll do that." Lainie closed the door behind her.

She made her way slowly down the steps, deliberately avoiding meeting the glittering depths of Rad's gaze. At the bottom of the steps she brushed past him, turning down the hallway toward the kitchen with Rad following. Once in the kitchen, she set the tray on the counter and began clattering the dishes into the sink, fighting the urge to hurl one of them at him. Rad merely leaned negligently against the counter a few feet away.

"So Lee Walters is still hanging around?"

There was a razor-sharp edge to his jeering voice that caused Lainie to glance up. The chilling indifference of his expression reminded her unwillingly of a coiled rattlesnake.

"He isn't 'hanging around,'" Lainie retorted sharply. "This is the first time I've seen him in years. Not that it's any of your business."

"You are still legally my wife."

"By whose choice?" She spun angrily around. "Not by mine, I can assure you. Maybe I got tired of all your threats of bringing false charges of adultery against me if I tried to sue for divorce. Maybe I've decided to make them real."

A cold shaft of fear pierced her as she watched Rad uncoil and move toward her, the rage glittering in his eyes. He halted inches away. Lainie saw the muscles move as he clenched his jaw while he successfully controlled his temper.

"You're wasting your time threatening me, Lainie. I wouldn't be the one to suffer the consequences of such an act." Rad was now icy cool and contemptuous.

She had long known the bitter truth of his statement. It would be she who suffered the degradation and not Rad. The utter futility of the situation washed over her.

"Why don't you just leave, Rad? We have nothing more to say to each other." Lainie suddenly felt exhaustedly tired. Speaking was an effort. "I've refused your offer. Even though I'm probably being ridiculously noble, at least let me keep some of my pride.''

"You can keep your pride." A muscle twitched near his mouth. "I don't know how long it will feed you or pay for the care that your mother is going to need. I didn't make an open-ended offer to you. If I choose to make a similar offer later, you can be sure the conditions will be different." His gaze roamed over her tear-brightened eyes and belligerent expression with analytical indifference. "I won't ask you to accompany me to the door. I'll find my own way out."

CHAPTER FOUR

REMOVING THE SAVORY BALLS of what had been leftover ham from the oven, Lainie placed them in a warmed serving dish. The fondue sauce of tomato, cheese and onions had already been reheated and was emitting its tantalizing aroma from its earthenware dish. She placed the chafing dish containing the sauce on its fondue burner and carried it into the living room, where the crunchy cubes of bread were waiting with the serving plates and wooden-handled forks. Returning to the kitchen, she untied the apron that had protected her cream pantsuit and adjusted the multicolored sash around her waist.

She had just left the kitchen carrying the dish of delicately spiced ham balls when the front doorbell rang. This time it had to be Lee, Lainie asserted silently. Her composure couldn't take another visit from Rad. Thankfully she didn't have to worry as she opened the door to the gentle smiling face belonging to Lee Walters.

"I thought I was supposed to be the one bearing gifts," he jested, sniffing appreciatively at the fragrant aroma coming from the dish in her hand.

"I made a fondue." Lainie explained unnecessarily. "I was just taking these ham balls into the living room when the doorbell rang."

"Do you suppose rosé wine goes with fondue?" Lee asked. There was a humorous tilt to his eyebrows as he withdrew the bottle of wine he had been holding behind his back.

"My mother always told me you could never go wrong with rosé wine. Why don't you take it on into the living room while I go get the glasses." Lainie laughed, then handed him the dish she had been carrying. "Here, take this, too."

Lee accepted it obligingly. The nonsensical conversation relaxed Lainie's nerves, still jumbled from Rad's visit. Not that anything was going to allow her to forget that he had come. That would be like asking for the moon. As she gathered the wineglasses together from their nook in the kitchen cupboards, she knew a sense of relief that Lee was going to keep her company this evening. The revelation of her own still vitally alive emotions where Rad was concerned had had a traumatic effect. It was frightening to learn that Rad still had the ability to make her respond so wantonly. Lainie was hesitant to dwell upon the reasons for this. The idea that she still might be in love with him was a thought that she didn't want to face.

That was the reason she allowed herself to be drawn into Lee's lighthearted air of frivolity. When she re-entered the living room she found Lee already sampling the savory meatballs liberally dipped in the fondue sauce. He had such an enchantingly guilty expression on his face, like a little boy just caught tasting the icing on a cake, that it made her feel young and carefree.

"You caught me snitching!" Lee reached out for the wineglasses and the corkscrew.

"I take that as a compliment that you couldn't resist my cooking," Lainie laughed, watching as he expertly opened the bottle of wine.

"Too true," Lee agreed. He poured equal portions of the light red wine into the stemmed glasses, handing one to Lainie and keeping one for himself. Then he raised his toward her in a gesture of a toast. "To many more delicious fondues, and many more bottles of wine, and to many more evenings with you."

It was difficult meeting his gaze, his blue eyes sparkling as brightly as the pale red wine. Lainie raised her glass in acknowledgment of the toast, knowing Lee had given it sincerely, yet not knowing how true she wanted it to be. Lee seemed to sense this, and with the understanding that Lainie admired so much in him, he immediately set forth to change that slightly serious tone. In minutes they were both attacking the light repast, dipping crunchy cubes of bread into the fondue sauce.

Later, their appetites replete, they jointly relaxed against the back of the sofa, Lee patting his tummy in satisfaction. He reached inside his suitcoat pocket and withdrew a silver cigarette case. He flipped it open and extended it to Lainie.

"No, thank you," Lainie refused. "I don't smoke."

Lee glanced significantly at the marble inlaid end table beside him and the crystal ashtray containing two cigarette butts. Unconsciously Lainie followed his gaze, the light color fading from her cheeks when she saw the object of his puzzling glance. Realizing that Lainie had noticed the reason for his inquiry, Lee felt he had to explain.

"I thought maybe you'd taken up the filthy habit," he jested. His expression plainly said that she didn't need to tell him who had been there.

Patting back any imaginary strands of hair that might have loosened themselves from her Gibson Girl coiffure, Lainie fought to control her rising tension. It seemed silly to conceal the fact that Rad had been there. Yet it was equally unnecessary to tell Lee of his visit. For five years she had tried to shut Rad out of her thoughts and her life. That hadn't succeeded. Perhaps the best course would be to treat the subject of Rad casually.

"Those are probably Rad's." She busied her hands collecting together the serving plates and forks, feeling Lee's gaze upon her, yet not ready to meet it. "He called in today."

She tried to make it sound like a natural thing, but Lee had been at the concert and he knew better. His hand reached out for her comfortingly. She watched the struggle in his face as he tried to find words to express his feelings. She smiled at

him reassuringly, letting him know that she had
escaped the confrontation nearly unscathed.

"I think that calls for a change of subject," Lee
exhaled slowly. "I'm sure it would be in bad taste
to express my blatant dislike of the man you were
once married to. So what do you say? How about
me helping you with the dishes?"

"That won't be necessary. I planned to stack
them in the sink and leave them till morning."

"It's hardly a romantic way to spend an evening," Lee admitted, rising from the couch and
extending a hand to Lainie. "But we can always
put on some music to do the dishes by and liven it
up."

Lainie hesitated before giving in to his captivat-
ing smile. "You find the record while I run
upstairs to check on mother."

Rad's name was not mentioned again the entire
evening. Lee set out to be amusing and succeeded,
drawing bubbly laughter from Lainie. It had been
so long since she had laughed like that that she was
sorry to see the evening end. He had not made her
feel in the least ill at ease, accepting without a
word her need to check on her mother at different
times in the evening, yet not bringing up her
mother's condition or expecting her to recount the
details of her illness. So if her good-night kiss
seemed overwarm and she lingered in his arms, it
was out of gratitude. It was only later in her room
alone that she wondered whether gratitude could
turn into love.

THE SUNLIGHT HOURS shortened and the wind shifted out of the northwest and the rocky Mountains. Summer had drawn to a close. The quaking aspens were turning to a golden shade so like the precious metal that came from the mountains. Mother Nature was having her one last fling, painting the countryside with rampant splashes of scarlet reds, golden yellows, and rusty orange, before Old Man Winter set in. The days became brisk and the invigorating air from the upper reaches of the mountains began turning noses and cheeks a healthy shade of pink.

It was a time of harvesting, of preparing for the winter ahead. The cut logs that had lain forgotten the summer long were suddenly being brought into homes to be used as fuel for the bright cheery fires. Children began dreaming of hobgoblins and witches and ghosts. Pumpkins became transformed into jack-o'-lanterns while luscious red apples were covered with caramel and stuck on a stick.

Clothes of lightweight synthetics and cotton were stored away and sweaters, tweeds, and woolens were shaken free of the mothballs that had lain dormant with them through the warm season. Tennis and swimming were replaced with talk of football, hunting, and speculation of snow. The perennially snowcapped higher regions of the Rockies had already received a fresh cover of snow. Winter itself was a cold breath away.

For Lainie, the autumn hadn't been a time for jubilant celebration. There was no time for making merry in anticipation of the cold months ahead. There had been hours enlivened with the presence of Lee or Ann, but for the most part her worries had increased. So gradually that even Lainie herself hadn't noticed it immediately, her mother's condition had worsened. The doctor's visits had become more frequent and his face had grown longer. New treatment was tried and failed. Lainie was beginning to feel that the only thing that increased were their debts. She could no longer make their monthly income match their monthly expenditure. Her mind had turned repeatedly to Rad's offer and her pride kept shutting the door. Although she had thought he might contact her again, he never did. She tried to be glad about that, but she wasn't.

Footsteps on the stairs interrupted her vigil in the kitchen. As she reached the door to the hallway, she was met by the portly figure of Doctor Henderson. His smile was grim and his eyes were sympathetic. In a fatherly gesture he put his hand on Lainie's shoulder and turned her back toward the kitchen.

"Make me a cup of coffee, would you, Lainie, and heavy on the sugar." The doctor settled his stout frame on one of the chairs at the table while Lainie filled his request.

She refilled her own stoneware cup and carried both to the table. Her acquaintance with Doctor Henderson preceded her mother's illness, going back to the time when her father was alive, so it was more than intuition that told her that the news he had was unpleasant. She watched his spoon make repeated trips to the sugar bowl as turned his coffee into a form of syrup.

"Strong and sweet," he smiled, sipping his coffee and smacking his lips in satisfaction. He glanced thoughtfully at Lainie. "Like you, little Lainie, but of course you're not little anymore. Like my German grandmother used to say, 'We grow too soon old and too late smart.' But I'm getting off the track," he sighed. "Your mother has deteriorated rapidly in the last couple of months. You only have two choices in front of you. Both of them will probably require hospitalization, or at the very least, round-the-clock nursing here at home."

"What do you mean by two choices?" Lainie asked. Her hands firmly circled the cup, needing the warmth to ward off the sudden chill.

"You've known for a long time that her condition was terminal. You've been a doctor's daughter too long for me to beat around the bush. Your mother is an eyelash away from the last phase." Doctor Henderson looked her squarely in the eye. "There's a chance—now just a chance—mind you, that if she is hospitalized, there's some new treatment being tried that may prolong her life for a few months and possibly reduce some of the pain she's suffering."

"And the other choice?" Lainie prompted.

"And the other choice is to let the illness take its

course. Her pain will increase and sedatives will no longer give her relief. And the results will remain the same. She'll die."

His blunt words turned Lainie's head down and away. It was a cruel game of Hobson's choice. Either door she chose would open to yawning blackness.

"I couldn't bear to watch my mother's face become twisted with the agony of pain," Lainie murmured. "I don't know where I'll get the money to pay for it, but I want her to have this new treatment."

The surgeon's hands reached out to cover Lainie's. "I wish you weren't so alone," he sighed, squeezing her hands before he rose from the table. "I'll make arrangements for her to enter the hospital the day after tomorrow."

CHAPTER FIVE

THE HOSPITAL CORRIDOR was bustling with nurses, technicians and aides. The green and gold tweed suit that Lainie wore, so perfectly tailored, suggested a wealth that she didn't possess as she walked beside her mother being wheeled down the corridor. The hopelessness of the situation had struck her forcibly after Doctor Henderson had left. The desire to flee from the responsibility her decision would bring was strong. But it had been a passing fear, one she could overcome. Looking down on her mother's wan face, Lainie knew her compassionate decision had been correct. Her mother was weak; therefore Lainie must be strong.

They had arrived at her mother's room. One of the aides was holding the door open. Lainie followed, glancing around at the other occupants of the room uneasily. One of the women smiled back at Lainie welcomingly. Another older woman was sleeping. The two aides were carefully shifting her mother from the cot to the hospital bed. The movement seemed to lift her mother out of the state of lethargy she had been in, and Lainie watched the dull blue eyes take in her surroundings. Then the frightened and questioning gaze was turned on the two aides.

"This isn't my room," her mother insisted with a weak yet imperious air. "You've taken me to the wrong room."

"I'm sorry, ma'am. This is where we were told to take you."

"It's a mistake." Mrs. Simmons's head moved fretfully against the pillow. "Somebody's made a mistake. Lainie, you must check on it at once."

"Yes, mother, I will." Lainie moved forward to still her mother's nervous fingers picking at the bed's coverlet.

"You know I always have a private room." It was a plaintive, protesting cry.

"We could pull the dividing curtains," one of the aides suggested gently.

"Would you, please?" Lainie replied, smiling at the thoughtful and considerate offer.

The beige curtains were pulled, but they did little to alleviate her mother's distraught condition. The younger aide smiled sympathetically at Lainie before the two of them wheeled the portable cot out of the room.

Lainie had known her mother would be upset when she discovered she would have to share a room with other patients. But the admissions clerk had been adamant when Lainie had requested a private room. The bills from her mother's previous hospitalizations had not yet been paid, although Lainie had made monthly payments toward them. The clerk had told her that the hospital didn't feel it would be fair to Lainie or to themselves to add the extremely high cost of a private room.

It was such a logical statement that Lainie couldn't argue against it. She had hoped to persuade her mother to become reconciled to other patients in the room, but the furtive glances that her mother was casting toward the unseen people beyond the curtain led her to believe it was a hopeless wish.

"I can't stand to have those people watching me," her mother whispered.

"But they can't see you," Lainie replied calmly.

"But they're just on the other side. I have no idea who they might be. They're complete strangers." She clutched Lainie's hand tightly. "You must do something."

Before Lainie could reply, the curtains were parted and a nurse in a sparkling white uniform and starched cap walked in. With an instinct born of long association with overwrought patients, the nurse immediately sensed the tension. She glanced briefly at Lainie before turning a bright, cheery smile toward the frail woman in the hospital bed.

"I'm Nurse Harris." The friendly voice was meant to put the patient at ease. "I see you've established your own private nook."

"There's been a mistake, nurse. I'm supposed to have a private room."

The urgent, almost sobbing statement brought a

startled glance from the nurse to Lainie, who gave a brief, negative shake of her head.

"Let's see, your doctor is Doctor Henderson," the nurse said as she consulted the chart at the end of the bed. "Perhaps you should discuss this error with him. He should be making his rounds shortly. I'm sure he'll take care of everything to your satisfaction."

This seemed to mollify Lainie's mother slightly. "It's just that you never know who's in the room with you." The snobbish ring in Mrs. Simmons's voice made the nurse's smile stiffen, while the color rose in Lainie's cheeks.

"They're all human beings in need of care," the nurse replied a trifle sharply. "Now if you'll excuse me, I have other duties. The doctor will be with you shortly."

"I certainly wish Lawrence would come," her mother whimpered, referring to Doctor Henderson, after the nurse had left the room.

Lainie seated herself in the chair alongside the bed. But it was nearly a quarter of an hour later before Doctor Henderson arrived. He was accompanied by a tall, slender, balding man with dark-rimmed glasses, introduced as Doctor Gordon, a specialist in the field of her mother's illness. The pair had barely begun their examination when Mrs. Simmons began complaining about being in the room with other patients. Doctor Henderson attempted to laugh off her fears, but it only served to make her increasingly nervous.

Leaving Doctor Gordon to continue the examination, Doctor Henderson motioned for Lainie to step out of the room with him. She quietly explained the hospital's position and he nodded understandingly but ruefully. Minutes later they were joined by Doctor Gordon.

"What seems to be the problem? Surely this hospital has a private room available?" he asked.

"It does," Doctor Henderson agreed. "But perhaps we could convince Mrs. Simmons to the contrary."

Then he went on to explain the situation to Doctor Gordon.

The specialist's reaction to the news was unfavorable. "I can appreciate your problems," Doctor Gordon addressed Lainie. "But unfortunately, if your mother's agitation persists, it may negate any progress these treatments might make."

THE MORNING MOVED to noon; the noon moved to afternoon; and the afternoon moved to evening. Despite Doctor Henderson's assertion that there were no private rooms available, Mrs. Simmons only became more distressed. He was forced to put her under heavy sedation before her nerves drove her to a progressively worse state of relapse. Lainie realized the only solution to the problem was money; but what few items at home that were of any value at all would not fetch enough money to make a dent in the hospital bill. If she had only accepted Rad's offer.... But she tried to banish that thought from her mind.

The magazine lay closed in her lap as she tried to think herself out of the situation. The lobby of the hospital floor was nearly empty. But Lainie wasn't interested in the other occupants, or the potted plants that were supposed to block out the clinical atmosphere, or the antiseptically clean, vinyl-covered sofas. She was so wrapped up in her dilemma that she didn't notice Ann or her husband Adam walk into the room followed by Lee Walters, and jumped convulsively when Ann's hand touched her shoulder.

"How's your mother?" Ann inquired as she settled in a seat beside Lainie.

"Not very good. She's sleeping, but they had to give her a sedative." Lee brushed her cheek with a light kiss that Lainie barely noticed.

"It's a good thing that we came tonight," Ann decreed, "to take you out of that pensive mood."

"Is anything seriously wrong?" The look in Lee's eyes mirrored the concern felt by all three at Lainie's serious expression.

"It's mother," Lainie sighed. "Being in a room with strangers makes her very nervous and our finances won't stretch to cover a private room. The specialist is afraid it might be detrimental to the treatments." A humorless laugh escaped her lips. "I guess I was hoping to conjure up a money tree."

Morosely grim glances were exchanged between

Ann and her husband. Lainie felt immediately chagrined that she had introduced a subject that not only was depressing, but also, so far, unsolvable. It wasn't fair to burden her friends with her problems.

"Before the storm clouds that are gathering over our heads break out with rain—" Lainie smiled brightly, if a little falsely "—I think we should leave. Shall we all go down to the coffee shop?"

"I think that's an excellent idea," said Lee, offering his arm to Lainie.

For almost an hour they sat around the table in the coffee shop, but their laughter and lighthearted attempts at conversation were stilted. The atmosphere around them was pierced with artificiality. The periods of tense silence grew more frequent as Lainie's face grew more drawn, the nagging worry pricking the back of her mind. After one prolonged silence, Lee's hand reached under the table and found hers. It was a comfort to know that he was standing by if she needed him.

"You're a lawyer, Adam!" Ann burst out suddenly. "Why couldn't Lainie sell the house?" She glanced apprehensively at Lainie, fearing her impulsiveness had put her nose in where it didn't belong. "I mean, after all, it is a large, rambling old house. It must be frightfully expensive to keep the old thing running, what with the cost of heating and all. It's in a good neighborhood, so it shouldn't be too difficult to sell it. It's probably a lousy suggestion," she ended lamely.

"No, it's not." The words of agreement were hesitant as Lainie spun the thought around in her mind, gradually warming to it. "I've suggested it before to mother. She could never bring herself to part with it, but now. . . ." Lainie couldn't bring herself to give voice to the fact that it was a possibility that her mother would never leave the hospital. "Is it possible, Adam?"

"Theoretically, yes," he agreed haltingly. "The house is solely in your mother's name?"

Lainie nodded that it was.

"Without checking further into it," he continued, "I would say that you'd either have to get your mother's permission or you'd have to have a doctor certify that she was physically incapable of handling her own affairs. In that case, the courts would probably allow you to act in her behalf."

"Then it could be done," Ann cooed with glee. Her eloquent blue eyes sparkled merrily at Lainie. "What luck that we have both a lawyer and a real estate man here! How fast would you be able to sell the house?" She turned eagerly toward Lee.

Ann's excitement was contagious. Lainie could feel the hope building inside her. It was as if the first star had been revealed in the dark evening sky. This suddenly seemed to be the answer to her problem. She, too, turned toward Lee hopefully, waiting anxiously for his opinion. But Adam wasn't finished.

"You understand this will take a certain amount of time." His cautious words were unwelcome and earned him a glaring look from his wife. "Not months, but certainly a few days."

Time was a factor, Lainie acknowledged inwardly. She didn't want to delay any longer than was necessary in finding a solution. Without being told, she knew it was essential to have her mother moved to a private room as soon as possible. She turned back toward Lee, looking for encouragement.

"I'd like to tell you I could sell the house tomorrow." His gaze was filled with compassion as he held hers. "But I can't. It's a case of supply and demand, and right now, the supply outweighs the demand."

"You mean you couldn't sell the house?" Ann cried out, knowing she had unwittingly raised Lainie's hopes falsely.

"I have no doubt I could sell the house—in time."

Her evening star turned into a shooting star that faded out of sight. Still Lainie's gaze clung to Lee's apologetic face, trying by force of will to make him relight her dream.

"It would be cruel to tell you differently," Lee continued. "It could take a day, a week, a month, or more. There's just no way to predict."

"That pretty well squashes that," Adam said grimly, throwing off the switch that had briefly brought light to Lainie's darkness.

"I refuse to give it up!" There was a suggestion of a pout around Ann's mouth. Her hand tugged at her husband's sleeve impatiently. "We can talk to our parents, persuade them to buy the house as an investment."

"No!" Lainie forcefully rejected such a plan. "I refuse to allow my friends to take that kind of risk. I'll find some other way to raise the money."

"But there isn't any other way," Ann protested. "What kind of risk would they be taking! After all, they would be buying the house."

"And it could turn into a white elephant, as it has for me."

Her decision was final. Further protests, mostly from Ann, couldn't change her from the course she knew to be right. The little etchings of relief around Adam's eyes when the decision was finally accepted made her glad that she hadn't given in to her friend's generosity. Rather than inflict any more gloom on the gathering, Lainie made the first move to leave, picking up her gold leather bag and rising from the table. The other three had no choice but to follow suit.

"Stop looking at me as if I were some lost, stray kitten tossed out in the blizzard," she teased as a very dejected Ann stared mournfully at her.

"But what are you going to do?" Ann persisted.

Lainie couldn't meet her friend's beseeching gaze. Another decision had been forming in her mind, but it still wasn't firm enough to bear up under the vocal abuse that Ann would give it. Her pride had stopped her once before, but under different circumstances. Now the situation was critical. And the question was whether she could afford to let her pride stand in her way again. The answer only she herself could give.

"I want to go check on mother again." Lainie reached out for her friend's hand. "I can't thank you all enough for what you tried to do."

"You make it sound as if we were offering some great sacrifice." Now it was Ann's turn to tease the solemn expression on Lainie's face. "When it's for people you care about, it's never a sacrifice."

"If you women are going to get sloppy, I'm going home," Adam announced.

"Men!" Ann sighed in exasperation, rolling her eyes significantly at Lainie. "I suppose I'll have to take him home."

Lee's arm encircled Lainie's waist as she exchanged a chorus of goodbyes with Ann and Adam. After they had left, her head rested just for a second on his shoulder, enjoying the comfort of his arms. When she glanced up to his gentle blue eyes, his adoration was there for her to see. She wished briefly that he would bestow one of those tender, warm kisses on her lips, but she knew his sense of propriety wouldn't allow him to give such a caress in a public place.

"How are you getting home?" he asked.

"I have the car," Lainie replied softly.

"Would you like me to follow you?"

"No, I don't know how long I'll be."

By unspoken agreement they left the coffee shop and headed toward the elevator that would take her to her mother's floor. He pushed the button and almost simultaneously the door to the elevator opened. Lainie stepped inside, then turned to face Lee. His hand reached out and captured a brown curl, and lingered on her cheek.

"If you need me...." he said softly.

Lainie smiled and nodded. His hand moved away and the elevator doors closed, blocking out the fair hair and the strong, silent face.

The curtains were still drawn, wrapping her mother in an insecure cocoon, but Lainie knew that the fitful drug-induced sleep could hardly be called restful. She stood for many silent moments at the foot of her mother's bed, staring at the still daintily feminine form and the lines of pain that creased the once perfect features.

Walking slowly out of the room, Lainie paused at the nurses' office, making sure that they had her telephone number in case she was needed during the night. Leaden feet carried her down and out to the parking lot where her car was parked. The person who climbed behind the wheel was an automaton of herself, mechanically making the correct turns that would take her home, while her conscious mind remained with her mother.

As she inserted her key in the front door lock, Lainie knew there was no way she could harden her heart to her mother's plight. Once inside, she leaned against the heavy oak door without bothering to switch on the light in the foyer. She made

her way through the half darkness to the door of
the den, opened it, stepped inside, and switched on
the light. Her eyes focused on the telephone on the
desk as she removed her coat and placed it with her
bag on the leather sofa. Never taking her eyes off
the black object, she walked around and seated
herself behind the walnut desk. Her heart kept saying tomorrow and her mind kept saying now. Her
hand reached out slowly, then almost snatched the
black receiver from its cradle. She was shaking all
over and the blood was hammering in her ears, but
she willed her trembling fingers to dial Rad's
number. Her hard-fought courage nearly deserted
her when Sondra answered the phone, yet somewhere she gathered the nerve to ask for Rad.

"Who should I say is calling?" The cold distaste
in Sondra's voice grated on Lainie.

"This is a personal call," she replied with the
same amount of coldness.

She sensed the hesitancy on the opposite end of
the line and realized there must have been just the
right air of authority in her own voice to make
Sondra unsure.

"I'll see if Mr. MacLeod is available." The line
went silent except for a distant mumble of voices.
The seconds seemed to be minutes and again
Lainie fought the desire to replace the receiver on
the hook.

"MacLeod here." Her heart lodged in her throat
at the sound of the masculine voice. "Hello?" Rad
repeated when Lainie failed to reply.

For a moment she was afraid she wasn't able to speak. Then finally she breathed, "It's Lainie."

This time there was silence on his end of the line. She thought he might have broken off the connection.

"Yes?" His voice was coolly impersonal.

"I . . . I wanted to discuss something with you," Lainie stuttered.

There was another pause. "I'll be free in half an hour. I'll send a car for you."

"No!" Her cry was instantaneous. She was suddenly afraid to face him. She wanted time to think before she met him again. "I mean, it's not that important. It can wait until tomorrow."

"In half an hour," Rad repeated firmly. Then the dial tone told her he had hung up. For ten minutes she tried to call him back, but the line was busy. Some inner sense told her that he had taken the phone off the hook, and that angered her. Rad knew her too well, therefore he wasn't going to give her the opportunity to back out once she had made the initial move. She could imagine the smug smile that must have been on his face when she identified herself. It was probably giving him immense satisfaction that she was the one who was running to him, after she had previously thrown his offer back in his face. If he thought she was coming there to eat humble pie, he was mistaken! She wasn't going begging with a lowered head. Lainie glanced down at her tailored suit and knew it didn't give her the sophistication and poise necessary to meet Rad.

There wasn't much time left before the car was due to arrive. Knowing Rad, it would be there promptly. Her mind was already picking out the dress she would wear as she hurried up the stairs to her room. It was a deep ocher gold knit with long sleeves and a cowled neckline. It molded the angles brought on by her loss of weight and changed them into curves. With it she would wear the fake leopard-skin coat with the black fur collar and hem, Lainie decided, removing it from her wardrobe along with the dress. With lightning speed she changed her clothes and freshened her makeup. She was just debating whether to put her hair up when the doorbell rang downstairs. She had no choice; she had to leave it down. It suited her better that way. Slipping the spotted coat over her shoulders, she dashed down the stairs. She took a deep breath to calm her racing pulse before opening the door. She expected to see Rad standing in the doorway, but he wasn't.

"Mrs. MacLeod?" the stranger in the blue uniform inquired.

"Yes," Lainie answered a trifle breathlessly.

The man extended his identification to her, which verified that he was Ralph Mason, employed by MacLeod Incorporated. "Mr. MacLeod told me to take you to him," he explained, moving to the side of the door so that Lainie could precede him to the black limousine parked in the driveway.

The chill that whispered over her skin had nothing to do with the brisk night air. It was caused

solely by her coming meeting with Rad MacLeod.
Perversely she wished Rad had met her instead of
sending someone in his place. She slipped into the
back seat, nodding politely at the man before he
closed the door behind her. The world outside the
car windows seemed an alien place with intermit-
tent beams of streetlights, blinding flashes of on-
coming car headlights, and blinking neon signs.
Occasionally people would be seen on the pavements, their mouths moving as they exchanged
conversation, but no sound penetrated the luxury
car. Lainie huddled deeper in the corner, pulling
the coat around her face so that the silky fine fur
brushed her cheeks.

Why was she going to see Rad? Hadn't he told
her that the offer might not remain open? Lainie
would rather have had their discussion take place
over the telephone, which was probably the reason
Rad had cut her off. He was no doubt deriving
some sadistic pleasure from having her make this
tension-filled journey across town so that he could
refuse to help her when she arrived. Another chill
of apprehension swept over her as she remembered
something else he had said.

"The conditions might not remain the same."
What could he have meant by that? If it was security or collateral he wanted, Lainie decided she
could always put up the house. The car made a
sharp turn, jerking her thoughts back to the present.

"Where are we going?" She glanced around,

not recognizing the route they were taking. "This isn't the way to the house."

"House?" The man's glance in the rearview mirror was curious. "Mr. MacLeod doesn't live in a house. He lives in an apartment. It's just a few more blocks, ma'am."

"I see." Lainie couldn't stop an embarrassing flush of color from filling her cheeks. "Has he lived there long?" She was startled by the news that Rad no longer lived in their house on the outskirts of Denver in the foothills of the Rocky Mountains.

"Since before I came," the chauffeur replied, "which is nearly three years ago."

There was a smile playing at the corner of the man's mouth, as if he were secretly amused that she didn't even know where her husband lived. But it was more upsetting to know that Rad hadn't bothered to tell her that he had moved. It would have saved her from making a fool of herself.

True to his word, minutes later the chauffeur halted the car under the canopied entrance of a tall building. Leaving the motor running, he got out of the car, walked around to Lainie's side and opened the door for her. The barest gleam of amusement was in his eyes as he motioned toward the large glass doors.

"The elevator is to your right, ma'am," he said. "The penthouse."

Lainie clamped her lips together tightly and nodded. The chauffeur touched his cap, walked back around the car and drove away. She walked slowly toward the doors, pushed them open and turned to the right toward the elevator. There she hesitated, knowing she could turn around and go home if she chose. But that wasn't the reason she had come. Once she had stepped inside the elevator and the doors had closed behind her, she stared unblinkingly at the top button that would take her to Rad's apartment. She pushed it quickly, hating the way her hand shook and hating even more the flutterings in her stomach. Silently she was zoomed upward and brought gently to a stop at the top floor.

The elevator doors stretched open and she stepped through into a richly paneled foyer accented by double doors of carved black walnut. Lainie felt as if she was going through an obstacle course. Her knees trembled as she ordered them to take her to the door. She pushed the button on the brass doorbell and heard the answering buzz sound inside the apartment. If Sondra was still there, she thought rebelliously, she would turn around and walk back out of the apartment.

There was a click and then the doors swung open. There was another stranger standing in front of Lainie. She nearly sighed in exasperation. She identified herself to the man in the black suit and he immediately stepped aside and allowed her to enter. At least Rad was not going to leave her standing in the foyer, she decided. The black walnut doors were closed behind her and she heard the click of a lock. She cast a startled glance at the man who had greeted her.

"We keep the doors locked at all times, ma'am," he explained. "Otherwise anyone could get into the elevator and come to the top floor, and gain entrance to the apartment without us knowing it."

Lainie knew she should have realized the logic in that, but it seemed as if her avenue of escape had been blocked. She didn't have time to dwell on the discovery, as the man was already walking ahead of her and indicating that she should follow. He paused at an open archway of a room.

"Mr. MacLeod will join you shortly," he said.

So she was destined to wait again. Lainie sighed, stepping into the room. Her suede heels made almost no sound as they sunk into the plush white carpeting. Her almond-shaped hazel eyes roamed over the room, stunned by the unusual color combination that was almost modernistic. Yet there was nothing really modernistic about the furnishings, only the colors that were used—white, gray, and black.

The walls were creamy white interspersed with beams of black walnut, with cross beams of black walnut on the ceiling. In the center of the opposite wall, flanked by floor-to-ceiling white draperies, was an enormous fireplace of richly polished gray stone. Two plushly cushioned sofas covered in matching gray velvet with large throw pillows of black and gray faced each other in front of the fireplace. Between them was a large rectangular coffee table, again of black walnut. Other plumply cushioned side chairs were in a deeper shade of gray, also accompanied by tables of black walnut. Scattered around the room were statues, a blend of contemporary and ancient design, but all of metal. Indirect lighting was concealed in the ceiling beams, adding to the cozy luxury and elegance of the room. The daring decor fascinated Lainie as she reveled in the spaciousness afforded by the light colors and the opulence of the lush materials. Yet piercing through the aesthetic facade of beauty was the reminder that this was essentially a masculine room. There was a quicksilver feeling of seductiveness and virility to it that made her apprehensive.

The back of her neck began tingling. Although she hadn't heard a sound, Lainie knew that Rad had entered the room. She steeled herself to remain calm as she turned to look at him. As she met his dark gaze, her determination was dissolving at the same pace as her legs. He was so compellingly handsome standing there just inside the archway, wearing black trousers that fitted tautly over his thighs.

But it was the rich coral-colored silk shirt with its bloused sleeves, wide-pointed collar and open neckline that complemented his own dark features and gave him an air of roguish good looks. The warm color of his shirt suddenly made the room come alive, pervaded by his vitality. Lainie turned back toward the fireplace as one side of Rad's mouth twisted with a humorless smile. She knew the color had left her cheeks, just as she knew that he had disturbed her more than she wanted to admit. She had to get control of herself, or flee.

Lainie was conscious again of Rad's movement. Without looking, she knew it was not in her direction. She grasped at these moments of reprieve. There was a tinkling of ice in glasses and the sound of pouring liquid. In her mind's eye she remembered the tiny alcove as she had stepped through the archway and the carved black walnut bar in its recesses. Then there was silence. Lainie cursed the carpeting that so completely muffled the sound of footsteps so that she had no way of knowing exactly where Rad was unless she looked. Thankfully there was the tinkling of ice in a glass just a few feet behind her, which warned her he was approaching. Now that she knew she had to fight her awareness of him, she was able to turn toward the sound with a hard grip on her emotions.

"You looked in need of something to drink." Rad extended toward her a classically simple glass of clear liquid brightened by a twist of lime.

Lainie took the glass hesitantly, carefully avoiding touching his hand. The sparkle in his eyes bespoke his amusement at her childish gesture. She moved away, sipping quickly at the drink and letting the potency of the vodka return the color to her face.

"Well?"

"It's a very beautiful room." Lainie knew that wasn't the response he wanted, but it was all she could say. She wasn't quite ready to tell him the reason for her visit, even though she knew he was aware of it.

"I'm glad you don't find it colorless." Rad was laughing at her.

Her nervous steps had taken her to the fireplace, where she was forced to turn around. Rad was sitting on the sofa, an arm stretched out across the back as he studied her with amusement. He was in command of the situation and totally at ease, and that knowledge made Lainie even more uncomfortable. The room seemed suddenly oppressively warm, and Lainie realized she was still wearing her coat. With an attempt at a poise she didn't feel, she unbuttoned her coat and shrugged it back across her shoulders.

"Mr. Dickerson!" Rad called out. Almost instantly the man who had greeted Lainie appeared in the doorway. "Would you take Mrs. MacLeod's coat?"

With a tight smile of discomfort, Lainie removed her coat and handed it to the man. Did nothing escape Rad's attention, she wondered in irritation. As the man walked out of the room carrying her coat, she wished for it back. It had given her a fragile sense of security that she could leave anytime she wanted to and provided another barrier from Rad's penetrating gaze.

"That will be all for this evening, Dickerson,"

said Rad as the man reappeared in the archway, and she glanced fearfully at Rad. Why had he dismissed the man when she was still here? "I didn't suppose you wanted servants listening in on our conversation," Rad answered her unspoken question with his usual perception.

The silence stretched out, allowing her tension to mount. Unwillingly she seated herself on the sofa opposite Rad. He was obviously waiting for her to bring the subject up, and she had no idea where to begin. Now she rolled the half-empty glass of vodka nervously between her hands.

"Mother was admitted to the hospital today," Lainie began hesitantly. "Doctor Henderson believes there are some new treatments that can help her. He's called in a specialist to assist him."

She stopped and stared at the unreadable expression on Rad's face. His lack of cooperation angered her. A little smile of understanding or a sympathetic glance would make it so much easier for her, but that was not his intention. Liquor splashed out of the glass as she shoved it onto the black walnut table.

"Isn't it enough that I came here!" she cried out. Her temper flared quickly to the surface. "And you know why I'm here, too."

His raised eyebrow sent her quickly to her feet. She walked hurriedly to the fireplace and paused in front of the blackened hearth as if to gather warmth from the dead ashes. Tears turned the back of her eyes and her breath came in quick gasps. Misery, humiliation, and pride warred with the sensible, logical side of her mind that asserted the need for Rad's help. A flash of color appeared beside her. Lainie turned her hurt gaze toward it.

"You've come to see if my offer is still open," Rad said calmly.

"I don't want your money!" The words were hurled out in a burst of pride.

"Ah, but your mother needs it," Rad replied smoothly. "Otherwise you wouldn't be here."

"You're insufferably arrogant!"

"That isn't exactly the attitude you should take when you're trying to get money from a man."

"What should I do?" Lainie asked sarcastically. "Grovel at your feet or kiss your hand?"

"It would be a novel experience," Rad replied with the same degree of composure as before, unmoved by her spitfire attack.

"Well, I won't do it. I won't!" Lainie turned away, despair taking the conviction out of her voice. "All I want from you is a simple yes or no. Either you will help me or you won't."

"But that's not all I want from you," Rad murmured softly. The strange statement brought Lainie's head around so that she was looking at Rad over her shoulder. There was an unidentifiable gleam in his eyes that brought a breathlessness to her. The glittering light seemed to be born of anger and cruelty, but there was something else there, too, and it was that that held her mesmerized. His hand reached out and twined a lock of her hair in his fingers.

"If. . . if it's collateral—" Lainie's voice was a husky whisper. "I could arrange to sign over the house to you."

A mirthless chuckle escaped Rad's lips. "That wouldn't begin to cover your debts. I'll help you, Lainie. . . ."

The sentence hung unfinished in the air. Lainie turned around to face him, a hint of relief in her eyes. Then the possessive way he was looking at her and his unfinished words brought a tightening in her stomach muscles. His gaze was drawing her into its unfathomable depths. She had to lower her eyes to escape it, although his magnetism still drew her closer.

The black curling hairs on his chest were revealed by the open neckline of his shirt, evoking a desire in Lainie to slip her hands under the silk shirt and feel the warmth of his skin and the hardness of his muscles as she had done so long ago. It was a heady thought, one that sent her reeling backward, away from him. The distance was still only inches.

"What do you want from me, then?" The question was really a plea to be released from her overwhelming awareness of him.

"I want back what has always been mine. What I already bought and paid for once. Fool that I am, I'm paying again." His words were clipped and harsh. Yet when Lainie glanced up, he was calmly studying the lock of her hair in his hand. Feeling her startled eyes on his face, Rad turned his thoughtful and determined gaze on her. "I want you, Lainie."

She stepped backward, twisting her head to remove her hair from his grasp. "It's absurd!" she breathed, blinking up at him with rounded eyes. Her statement seemed to amuse him.

"You are still legally my wife," Rad pointed out. "All I'm asking is that you take up those duties once more."

The idea was ludicrous, Lainie thought wildly. She should reject it out of hand. Why was she hesitating? Why didn't she speak up? Why didn't she say she would never agree to those kind of conditions?

"And in return you'll—" Was that really her voice speaking so calmly?

"I'll pay all your debts and any future costs due to your mother's illness." He watched the conflicting emotions flit across Lainie's face.

The knowledge that Rad had all the cooks, housekeepers, and servants that he could possibly want left only one position for her to fill. Lainie had never realized he regarded her with such contempt. How could he be so cruel, she wondered. The tears overflowed her eyes.

"No!" Her voice was choked but clear.

"Don't try to convince me that you find me repulsive." Rad reached out, grasping her wrist and pulling her toward him so that her hands with their curling fingers were resting against his chest. "You tremble like a frightened kitten in my arms, but you'll just as quickly purr."

That was a fact that she knew too well to be true, and it made her much too vulnerable. "Have you suddenly grown tired of Sondra?" Lainie lashed out with the only weapon she had left, a spiteful tongue.

But Rad seemed to expect it. His dark eyes danced with devilish mischief. "Sondra has always been very satisfactory—in every respect."

"Then why do you want me?" she moaned, feeling a surge of old jealousy quake through her.

"Isn't it obvious?" A muscle at the corner of his mouth twitched involuntarily. "I still find you desirable."

"Oh, Rad," she murmured, gazing beseechingly into his face. "Do you hate me that much, that you would degrade me in that way?"

"Surely it's a more inviting a proposition than selling yourself in the streets," he jeered. He tightened his hold when she would have pulled away in shame.

"You know I never meant that," she whispered, hanging her head.

"Of course. I know also part of you wants to be my wife again."

"No!" Her whispered protest was accompanied by the horrifying discovery that what he said was true.

She was crushed tightly against his chest. His

shirt cast a rippling sheen over his muscles. The blood pounded in her head as she fought to control the urge to put her hands around his neck and bury her face in his arms in submission. The longing was intense; she closed her eyes to block it out. Brief seconds flitted past while his gaze studied her frightened face, then he released her swiftly and stepped away, snapping a lighter to his cigarette.

"That's my offer. Take it or leave it." His back remained turned to her as he spoke. He didn't glance around to see her reaction. Instead he picked up his empty glass and walked to the bar.

Lainie watched him as he refilled his glass and gulped it down. Her mind decreed that she was glad he had walked away, but her traitorous heart was crying. She was torn in two; one part of her was inflicting darts in the broad back covered by his silk shirt, while the other part wanted to rush over and throw her arms around him. What a fool she had been not to accept his previous offer! But that refusal had been dictated by her pride. Now need had replaced pride. What frightened Lainie now was that this need for Rad had nothing to do with her mother. She still loved him. And she was beginning to wonder if she had ever stopped.

"For how long?" From out of her chaotic thoughts came the calmly worded question.

Rad poured himself another drink, turned to lean against the bar, and regarded her cynically, the glass in his hand. There was a raking thoroughness in his gaze that seemed to strip away all her carefully erected barriers. She wanted no time limit, no set day when she would be forced to renounce her love for him. Judging by the frown gathering on his forehead, her question was posing a problem to him.

"When I tire of you, I suppose."

"When will that be—a day, a week, a month, a year?" Pain etched bitter edges to her words.

"Would you prefer that I use the day of your mother's funeral as the termination of our agreement?" Rad sneered. "That might be appropriate. Since you're sacrificing yourself on her behalf. Then you could rejoice at being released from two tyrants."

Lainie flinched as the cruelty of his tongue lashed out at her. "That's unfair!" she breathed.

"Unfair! I'm keeping the width of a room between us while you make up your mind." Lainie turned away under his contemptuous glance. "I could have taken advantage of you a minute ago. All I had to do was kiss you a few times, murmur the right things in your ear, and you would have resisted me just long enough to sweeten your submission. That was what you wanted me to do, to make it easy for you to agree to my demands so that later you could throw it up in my face that I'd seduced you. If you agree to stay with me, it won't be due to any physical influence from me." Rad paused, his evenly measured gaze holding Lainie's. "So what's it going to be? Do you stay or do I call a cab?"

Lainie had to admit that he was right. A few minutes ago, if he had begun making love to her she would have agreed to anything and never been sure that the decision was her own. Now of her own free will she knew she wanted to go back to Rad. But he had stated his case so coldly and callously that she didn't know if she could.

"You make it sound so cheap and degrading." She made a small half turn away from him, lifting her blurred eyes toward the unseen heavens.

"Are you agreeing?" Rad's voice came from only a few feet away.

"God help me, yes!" There was a choked sob in her voice as she wondered what kind of purgatory she was committing herself to.

The touch of his hand upon her shoulders was light but firm as he gently turned her around toward him. She refused to lift her gaze and see the triumphant glitter in his eyes. Yet when his hand cupped her chin and forced her to look up into his face, she found herself staring into two dark pools of still water that were etched with tenderness.

"I will not degrade you," he said quietly. "You're the only woman I ever wanted as my wife and you will receive the honor and respect of that position."

He slowly folded her into his arms, his hand entangling itself in the thickness of her dark hair. Lainie wished he had spoken of a love he had once felt for her, but she had to be satisfied with his handing her back a little of her dignity. Rad held her tightly against him until some of her rigidity faded away and the warmth of his body had melted the coldness that had surrounded her heart. Lainie didn't resist when his mouth moved down over her hair, her closed eyes, to settle on her lips. Her hands even managed to encircle his neck and cling to him with bittersweet urgency as he lifted her off her feet and carried her into his bedroom.

There was a fleeting glimpse of rich royal blue draperies contrasting with the white carpet before Rad snapped the light out. He paused beside the bed, still holding her in his arms, his expression as he gazed at her unreadable in the darkness. He set her gently on the dark-colored bedspread. Very faintly she heard him murmur her name before he joined her.

THE SATIN SHEETS felt smooth to her skin and Lainie snuggled deeply into this unaccustomed luxury. Then the faint aroma of a man's cologne drifted past her nose. She blinked herself awake and the knowledge of where she was came back to her. Her eyes immediately went to the empty space beside her and the hollow place on the next pillow where Rad's head had lain. She reached out and touched the smooth sheet beside her, remembering the feeling of being whole again that she felt last night. She rolled over on her back, stretching her arms above her head, and studied this room that belonged to her and her husband alone. Her toes curled at the thought.

Again the walls were in white, as was the carpeting, but this time there were vivid splashes of blue that added vitality and zest to the room.

But nothing could match the zest that had come into her own life. Loving someone breathed a whole new life into her body. Her senses were heightened, freed of previous dullness and apathy. Her mind was more aware of the wonderful things in life, the precious beautiful things that you cherish rather than possess. But most of all, her heart was fulfilled and happy.

The hands on the clock on the dresser said it was half-past eight. Lainie wondered where Rad was, hoping he hadn't left for his office. His lovemaking last night had told her he wasn't totally immune to her. She had grown up a great deal since their last disastrous attempt to make their marriage work, and now she knew she had outgrown the childish possessiveness that had ruined it before. Perhaps if she tried this time to show that she was an understanding and loving woman, she would be able to win Rad's love....

A knock on the door interrupted her musings. Assuming it was Rad, she quickly rearranged her pillow, leaning against the back of the bed and pulling the covers closer around her chest. Her voice was eager as she bade the person to enter. But the door was opened by a woman in her late forties; a crisply starched green dress covered her stout figure and she regarded Lainie with a briskly intimidating expression on her face. She marched on into the room, carrying a tray.

"Mr. MacLeod thought you'd like breakfast." The words were snappish, plainly indicating that the woman was on the offensive. "It's not normally my duties to see that breakfasts are served in bed."

"I don't normally care for breakfast in bed." Lainie soothed the housekeeper's ruffled feathers. "But it was terribly thoughtful of Rad to suggest it. Would you put the tray over on the table by the window?"

There was a derisive sniff by the housekeeper, which brought a smile to Lainie's lips. This household wasn't accustomed to having a woman around, she realized. The servants were not likely to take kindly to a woman who appeared out of the blue, declaring herself to be Mrs. MacLeod. She would have to tread lightly at first.

"I don't know your name," she said as the housekeeper was about to leave the room.

"It's Mrs. Dudley," the woman retorted.

"It's nice to meet you, Mrs. Dudley," Lainie smiled. The woman nodded and reached for the doorknob. "Has my—has Rad left for the office?"

"No, ma'am." Mrs. Dudley's eyes glinted at her brightly. "Miss Gilbert arrived a little before eight. He's in the den with her now."

With that the woman left the room. Lainie felt a cloud gathering over her head. A light blue satin robe lay on a nearby chair. By the size of it, it belonged to Rad. Lainie reached out from beneath the covers and drew it toward her. She slipped into it quickly, rolling up the sleeves that tried to cover her hands. She walked around the bed to the table where the breakfast tray sat. Brushing her long hair behind her ears, she poured herself a cup of coffee, ignoring the eggs, bacon and muffins on the gold-rimmed china plate. She lifted the cup to her mouth in an involuntary movement while holding back the knobby linen curtain of blue and looking out at the city below.

The moment of elation had passed. Lainie was once more Rad's wife, but the old obstacles were still there, including Sondra Gilbert. The break in her heart that she thought had been mended by Rad's tenderly ardent lovemaking seemed to have broken open again. Nothing was as simple as she had painted it earlier. True, she was more understanding, more cognizant of the demands Rad's business placed on him, and more adult when it came to dealing with a relationship between them. The city with all its tall buildings and concrete roads stared back at her, exposing the harsh realities. If only she could understand why Rad had wanted her back! If it were only for physical satisfaction, then was there really much chance that she would be able to make their marriage last? What would happen if he tired of her?

"Good morning. Mrs. Dudley told me you were up."

Lainie looked over her shoulder as Rad entered the room. Not more than ten minutes ago she would have run to greet him. Now, as she stared at the imposing figure in the dark business suit, she feared the rejection that such a gesture might bring into his eyes.

"Good morning," she murmured in return. Her bland response brought a questioning look in his dark eyes.

Lainie turned back to the window, sipping her coffee rather than let his eyes probe into her momentarily confused emotions. Rad walked around the bed and paused in front of the table where Lainie's breakfast tray sat.

"Your food is getting cold."

"I don't really have much of an appetite this morning." Her stilted words betrayed her uncertainty about their new relationship.

This was getting her nowhere. They were exchanging polite conversation like two strangers. Lainie let the curtain fall back, shutting out the city.

"Rad, why did you want me back?" The question that had been uppermost in her mind was blurted out without conscious effort.

"Why do you think?" His voice came back sharply.

"I don't know." Lainie's eyes blurred as she stared at the coffee cup in her hand. "Maybe you wanted revenge for that girl you married who hadn't grown into a woman. I know I hurt and disappointed you all those years ago. I also know that physically you still want me." Her voice trembled and she tried to steel herself to remain composed. "And I'm not totally immune to you, either."

She wished she hadn't turned and looked at Rad's face. It possessed the unfeeling coldness of stone.

"But let me finish it for you," Rad inserted sharply. "What better method of revenge than to take you back as my wife and subject you to the humiliation of being in my debt?"

"Is that really the reason?" Her gaze begged him to deny it.

"You're a very clever girl, Lainie, to figure it out all by yourself." There was no mistaking the sarcastic sneer in his voice. "What other reason could there have been? I suppose I could have been so desperately in love with you that I wanted you back under any circumstances."

"But you never were in love with me," Lainie admitted unwillingly.

"No, I never was, was I?" His cold agreement lacerated her heart. "Now that we've aired all those unpleasantnesses, shall we get down to business?"

"Business?" Lainie echoed, cocking her head to one side in bewilderment.

"Yes, business," Rad snapped. "Sondra was over this morning so I could give her a list of the creditors who were to receive payment. Here it is." He passed a sheet of paper to her. "See if we've missed anyone."

Lainie accepted the paper with sort of a dazed look on her face.

"Naturally Sondra's first stop will be the hospital. I believe there was a question as to whether or not your mother could afford a private room."

With a trembling hand Lainie handed him back the paper. She wished she had never brought up the subject of why she was back with him. For one ridiculous moment she had thought it was for a reason other than the one he had stated. But Rad had let her know that affection had not been a part of his decision. She felt his eyes stray over the blue dressing gown she wore. Her pale cheeks filled with color as his gaze lingered on the low V neckline where the cleavage of her breasts was visible.

"The next thing on the agenda," he went on, "is to take you to your home where you can pick up some of your things."

Any thought that she might have looked seductively quaint in her attire was quickly doused.

"If you don't intend to eat your breakfast, I suggest you get dressed so we can leave."

"Don't you have to go into the office today?" Lainie asked, surprised by his implication that he would be accompanying her.

"One of the few benefits of owning your own company is that you can take rare days off by delegating authority to others in charge. You'll probably want to stop at the hospital, so I'll tell Mrs. Dudley we won't be in for lunch."

"Why are you taking me?" She couldn't stop herself from asking.

"To be perfectly honest, Lainie—" Rad stopped in front of the doorway "—and this seems to be a morning for honesty, I think you're getting cold feet. Let's just say I'm tagging along to make sure you stick to our bargain."

"I told you last night I would stay. I'll keep my word." Her chin lifted with pride.

"Sometimes the light of day changes people's minds. I recall another promise you once made— 'till death do us part.' "

"You made the same vow, Rad, along with 'to love and cherish,' " Lainie flared out quickly, her words ending in a choked sob.

"You were the one to walk out. That decision was entirely your own."

The door closed sharply behind him.

CHAPTER SIX

LAINIE WANTED TO HURL HERSELF onto the bed and give way to the storm of tears welling up inside her. There seemed to be no way to reach Rad. It was unbelievable that she could have fallen so deeply in love with a man who only regarded her with contempt and amusement.

"Where is the rainbow, daddy?" the child in her cried out. "Where is the end of the storm?"

A cold towel had done wonders to brighten her eyes and bring color to her cheeks. A single lipstick was the only makeup in her purse, but the scrubbed look suited her mood. Lainie fluffed the ends of her hair, grateful for the natural body that kept its bounce.

Satisfied with her appearance, she stepped out of the bedroom wearing the gold knit dress from the evening before. She paused in the living room, half expecting to see Rad there. There was no indecision in her movements; her step revealed the controlled sophistication that had been trained to appear natural. She realized that Rad was probably still in his den and she had no intention of opening doors trying to find him. Nor did she in-

tend to wait like a patient dog until her master came
for her. She walked determinedly through the archway to the small foyer that led to the black walnut
doors and the elevators. Almost immediately the
man who had greeted her the night before appeared.

"Dickerson, isn't it?" Her tone was authorita-
tive, altogether fitting for the new mistress of the
household. "Would you get my coat and tell Mr.
MacLeod that I'm ready to leave."

Minutes later Dickerson returned, carrying her
imitation leopardskin coat. "Mr. MacLeod will be
here directly."

Her smile was coolly polite as she accepted Dickerson's assistance in donning her coat. Her mask
was firmly in place and she couldn't afford the
slightest warmth to put a nick in it. But the man
didn't seem to expect it as he silently withdrew
down the hallway.

There was only the smallest wait before Rad
joined her. His mocking politeness grated on her
already raw nerves as he opened the door for her
and allowed her to precede him into the elevator.
Lainie refused to allow him to occupy even a corner of her side vision. She didn't even spare him a
glance when, once they were outside, he opened
the door of his Mercedes Benz for her. Only when
he, too, had slid into the car did she break the self-
imposed silence.

"I'd like to see my mother first," she said calmly.

"Whatever you say," Rad shrugged indifferent-
ly.

"THERE ARE A FEW FORMS that still need to be filled out," Rad told her after they had arrived at the hospital and were in the lobby. "So I'll be in the administration office for a while."

Lainie nodded grimly.

"You should check at the reception desk to get your mother's new room number. I imagine she's been moved by now."

Rad was right. Her mother was safely installed in a private room on another floor, and the change in her attitude was almost miraculous. Her smile was bright and cheery and there were no more fearful glances over her shoulder when Lainie arrived in her room. Doctor Henderson had already been there on his morning rounds.

The improvement in her disposition was so noticeable that Lainie didn't even want to contemplate discussing the change in her relationship with Rad. A glossed-over explanation that there were things to be done at home seemed to satisfy her mother. Lainie was able to withdraw from the room before Rad was able to come up. The time for explanations would come later.

Although her heels clicked loudly in the hospital corridor, Lainie was unconscious of her surroundings. In her mind she was caught in a maze and no matter which way she turned she couldn't get out. She never even noticed the man and woman standing at the nurses' office door when she walked past. The voice that called out for her to stop was from another world and she kept on walking. Then she was seized roughly by the shoulders and spun around.

"Lainie! Oh, my God, where have you been!" Lee Walters's blue eyes raced over her face and the upper portion of her body as if making sure she was unharmed. "I've been worried sick about you!"

Lainie stared at his hair, incredibly tousled as if he had been running his fingers through it. There was no mistaking the concerned expression on his face that was now becoming tinged with relief. He glanced around him, suddenly becoming conscious of the public display he was making, and quickly led her to the secluded waiting area. It was then that Lainie noticed that Ann was there, too.

"What are you doing here? What's happened?" Lainie queried, noting the concerned expression that was also on Ann's face.

"Trying to find you," snapped Ann.

"I've been out of my mind with worry," said Lee. The shaky edges of his voice confirmed that.

"I don't understand," Lainie said, looking from one to the other in confusion. "Why were you looking for me?"

"I called you last night, to make sure you'd arrived home safely," Lee started to explain, "but nobody answered your phone." The awful realization began to dawn on Lainie. "I wasn't concerned at first because I thought you'd stayed at the hospital a while longer, but I kept calling and there was still no answer. I checked with the hospital, thinking you'd possibly decided to stay all night with your mother, and they told me you'd left earlier.''

"And of course he couldn't get hold of us because we have an unlisted number,'' Ann put in.

"I thought perhaps you'd gone over to her house to spend the night rather than stay in your house alone,'' Lee explained.

"So he was camped at our doorstep at eight o'clock this morning.'' There was a nervous laugh as Ann tried to make light of the situation. "That's when he really became concerned—and me, too, as far as that goes. But darling Adam was still there. He made a few phone calls to make sure you hadn't been involved in some accident, then we came here to the hospital.''

"I'm so terribly sorry I've put you through all this,'' Lainie apologized sincerely.

"As long as you're all right—'' Ann smiled at her warmly ''—it doesn't matter. How did you manage to get your mother a private room? We were so shocked when we got here and found she'd been moved.''

"Where were you last night?'' Lee persisted in the previous line of questioning.

Lainie glanced from one to the other with a slightly panicked expression on her face. Explanations were being demanded and she wasn't ready to make them yet. Lee was still holding her arm possessively. Lainie moved uncomfortably out of his grasp. Lee's piercing blue eyes quickly picked up the flush in her cheeks.

"Where were you, Lainie?" he repeated, but more grimly this time.

"When...when...I got home last night—" the mounting heat in her face made speaking difficult "—I...I called Rad."

The expressions on both their faces told of their astonishment, except that Lee's was tinged with outrage. He moved convulsively toward her, then stopped. Lainie faltered, trying to find a way to break the news to both of them. She doubted if either one of them would understand, any more than she did.

"I thought he would help me. I couldn't think of anyone else to turn to."

"MacLeod!" Lee snorted derisively. "How could you bring yourself to go to him?"

"Rad had offered to help me once before," Lainie told him, her head tilted back defensively. "At the time I was too proud to accept it, but now I needed it."

"Judging by the fact that your mother now has a private room," Ann inserted, the only one gaining composure, "I guess we can assume he agreed to help you."

"Yes, he did," Lainie answered. Now was the time to tell them both that she had gone back to him, but the words wouldn't come out.

"If you called him on the phone and talked to

him, then why weren't you there when I called?"
Lee persisted.

"I called him, yes, but I had to go over to his
apartment to talk to him about it."

"You did what?" Lee seized her again roughly
by the shoulders.

"Lee!" Ann placed a restraining hand on his
arm. He immediately released Lainie, running a
hand through his tousled hair.

"Well, you could have waited until the morning," he growled. His agitation carried him a few
steps away from Lainie. "You didn't have to go
over in the middle of the night."

"It wasn't the middle of the night," Lainie inserted quickly. "It was early evening."

"Then where were you the rest of the night?
How long did you stay, for heaven's sake?" His
possessive attitude was beginning to rankle Lainie.

"That is none of your business!" she retorted
sharply.

The solitary sound of two hands clapping shattered the tension in the room. All eyes turned in its
direction. Rad was standing in the doorway, his
amused gaze taking in their startled glances.

"I was wondering how you were going to dodge
that question, Lainie," he laughed, moving forward to join them.

"What are you doing here, MacLeod?" Lee almost shouted.

Rad raised his eyebrow at Lee's loss of control,
but ignored the question. "You might be inter-

ested to know, Walters, that it was after nine o'clock this morning before Lainie left my apartment."

Lee's face was mottled with ill-concealed rage as he turned his accusing glance on Lainie. "Is that true?"

Lainie was only able to nod her head that it was.

Lee paced back and forth across the room like a caged lion, and Lainie was stunned by his display of emotion from a man who always seemed so implacable. His hand continually massaged the back of his neck as he fought to control his temper.

"If you'd only told me how desperate you were—if I'd only known that you—" His hands lifted toward her in a hopeless gesture. "My God, Lainie, I wanted to marry you!"

"Since she's never been divorced from me, that would have been a small miracle," Rad inserted, drawing a dark look from Lee.

"I guess there's no need to ask if that's true." His piercing blue eyes were cold crystals of ice as they turned on Lainie. "And I always thought you were so virtuous! You really were serious that night at the concert when you said you'd sell yourself in the streets!"

"If you want to leave this room standing up, you'd better apologize to my wife." Rad snapped savagely. Lainie wasn't the only one to glance in surprise at the man bristling by her side.

"I will apologize, but not because of any threat from you, MacLeod." There was a softening in

Lee's eyes as he turned toward Lainie. "Those words were spoken by a man who just lost the only woman he ever wanted. I wanted to hurt back. Your loyalty and concern for your mother didn't deserve that kind of attack."

"I understand," Lainie murmured, recognizing the pain that Lee was going through.

"I hope you do. Because if you ever need me—" his gaze carried a hostile challenge to Rad "—I'll be there, Lainie."

Lee turned sharply on his heel and left the waiting room. A sideways glance at Rad as he stared after the retreating figure revealed the fury that still seethed inside him. Ann stepped forward hesitantly, her rounded blue eyes taking in the strained look on Lainie's face and the grim one on Rad's. Lainie wanted to smile, but she was afraid it would crack her control.

"Listen, I'd better go." Ann's voice was uncertain and apologetic. "Call me in a few days."

"I will," Lainie promised.

Then she and Rad were left alone. Rad reached inside his suitcoat pocket and withdrew a pack of cigarettes, shaking one out and offering it to her, and she accepted with trembling hands. When she bent her head to the flame, she felt his burning gaze on her and she felt all the more uncomfortable. She turned, running her fingers through her hair and pushing it back from her face in a nervous gesture.

"How's your mother?" Rad asked as she continued to refuse to meet his eyes.

"She's fine."

"How did she react when you told her we were back together again?"

"I didn't tell her."

"And just when do you intend to spread the glad tidings to her?" Rad asked sarcastically.

"Soon," Lainie sighed. She cast him a sideways glance.

"Are you ready to leave?" he snapped, snubbing his cigarette out in the ashtray.

WHEN THEY ARRIVED at her home nearly three-quarters of an hour later, Lainie was glad to escape the constricting confines of the white Mercedes Benz. The deafening silence between them had been intolerable, but not any more so than the prickling awareness in her senses of his closeness. She had wished he would stop the car, gather her into his arms, and hold her tightly against his lean hard body. But his fingers had remained gripping the wheel and his attention was on the traffic. For all the notice that he paid her, the seat beside him could have been empty.

When Lainie extracted the key to the front door from her purse, Rad took it from her, inserted it in the lock, opened the door and replaced the key in his own pocket. He preceded her into the house, shrugging off his dark overcoat and tossing it over the stairwell railing. Rad knew she would follow him into the house and close the door behind them. He was the puppeteer and she was the puppet. Lainie studied the wide shoulders, wondering why and how she had fallen in love with this cold and complicated man.

"Will you be long?" Rad turned toward her suddenly.

"No, not long," she answered, moving quickly away from his gaze and toward the stairs.

"I have some calls to make. I'll be in the den."

The first thing that Lainie did upon reaching her room was to change from the gold dress to a pantsuit of rusty orange. From a drawer she took an autumn-hued scarf and folded it into a wide band to secure the hair away from her face, tying it at the back of her neck and letting the long tails of silk mingle with her own hair. The tips of her lashes she touched with mascara and brushed a peach pink blush onto her cheeks. Then she removed her suitcases from the cupboard and began the task of packing her clothes. She wouldn't allow her mind to dwell on anything other than the mechanics of her work, precisely folding each garment and laying it neatly in the opened cases.

Rad appeared in the doorway, briefly lounging against its frame before walking on into the room. Lainie paused, glancing up into his stonily carved features as if thinking she could find a reason for his presence, but the only thing she could see was a hint of impatience. Rad walked restlessly around the room, stopping occasionally to lift back a curtain and gaze out the window, or to flick his cigarette ash into an ashtray. His tension transmitted itself to Lainie.

"You don't have to worry about packing everything." Rad stopped in front of her dressing table, examining the articles on top of it. "I've opened charge accounts at various stores in town in your name. You'll want to update your wardrobe."

"That wasn't necessary," Lainie murmured.

"I'll be the judge of that." There was a leashed violence about him that sent a tremor quaking through her. "I'm sure you have some idiotic notion that I'm going to lock you in my bedroom like a prized jewel, but I assure you there will be several functions that you will have to attend—social functions where you'll be expected to dress in the style that would befit my wife."

"I'll do my best to see that I don't embarrass you." The implied criticism brought out Lainie's bitterness and resentment.

"Then I suggest you start wearing this again." With all the silence of a stalking panther, Rad was at her side, taking her left hand and roughly shoving her wedding ring on her third finger. Lainie's eyes flew to the open jewelry box on her dresser, where he had been standing. Her gaze was caught and held by his, a captive the same as her hand.

"I'm surprised you haven't sold it before now."

"I meant to send it back to you," she said.

"I'm glad you didn't." His lips twisted cynically. "It saves me from having to buy you another one."

"Can't we stop baiting each other this way?" With an effort Lainie broke free from his gaze and his hold, shutting the filled suitcase in front of her and locking it securely.

"Is that everything?" His cutting words snipped off her previous question.

"Just about. I have—"

"I'll send someone around to get the rest," Rad cut her off sharply. "I booked a table for one o'clock lunch. It's time we were leaving."

The restaurant where they lunched was a relatively new one that Lainie had never been to before. Yet it resembled other such establishments that catered to the executive class. Its decor was tastefully elegant, using wood paneling for a more masculine appeal. There were liberal touches of live foliage, either potted trees and ferns or climbing vines, as well as secluded tables cordoned off with deeply carved posts.

Rad had ordered for her, and only after the waiter had left did he ascertain whether his choice was to her taste. It was a rhetorical question, since Rad had always been well informed about her likes and dislikes. The food when it arrived was excellent, although the non-existent conversation at the table did little to stimulate her appetite. Lainie was glad when Rad signaled the waiter to bring their coffee, knowing it meant an end to this unpleasant meal. She accepted the cigarette he offered readily, realizing she couldn't bear another ten minutes of silence without occupying her hands with something.

"You've evidently seen a great deal of Lee Walters in these last few months." Rad's statement brought Lainie's head up with a jerk, not so much because of the ending of the silence but because of the ominous quiet in his voice.

"Yes, I have." Lainie inhaled on her cigarette deeply. She deliberately exhaled the smoke so that it would make a cloud between them.

"Did you know how he felt about you?"

"Yes." Her teeth bit off the end of the word as she guessed the purpose of this cross-examination.

"And what are your feelings toward him?"

The cigarette smoke began dissipating into the air and she no longer had a barrier between her and his searching eyes.

"Does it really matter?" she asked bitterly.

His expression became grim and forbidding. The words were already forming on her lips to deny that Lee meant anything more than a friend. Then she remembered how certain Rad had been of her last night; how sure he had been that after a few minutes in his arms she would capitulate to anything he requested.

"I've grown very fond of Lee. It was an affection that was in the growing stages." She marveled at the way she was able to meet his eyes so easily. "Given time, it probably would have matured into love." A bittersweet smile played at the corner of her mouth. "A quiet, comfortable love, like the warmth of a fire in a cold world, something you could snuggle up to. I always felt safe with Lee. He was a haven, dependable, always there when I needed him. I could always count on him to protect me, to stand up for me."

The glint in his eye reminded her that it had been Rad who had sprung to her defense, and Lee had been the one who had attacked her. She regretted her choice of words.

"And you don't believe I would protect you?" He mocked her openly.

"With you, I always have the feeling I'm hanging over the edge of a precipice and no one is there to rescue me." Lainie refused to let his amusement daunt her. "You're quite capable of protecting me from everything but yourself."

"And after last night—" his half-closed eyes roamed over the upper portion of her body with a thoroughness that seemed to strip away her clothing; a burning rush of color filled her cheeks "—after last night, you still want to be protected from me?"

With a slightly lurching movement Lainie rose from the table, feeling like a wild animal trying to flee from its captor. She grabbed her brown leather coat, which she had substituted for her leopardskin one, and dashed out of the room, knowing that Rad would be delayed from following her by taking care of their bill. She hated the knowing look that had been in his eyes, but not nearly as much as she hated herself for giving him the knowledge to put it there. Outside she glanced frantically around for a taxi, but there was none in sight. She had taken two steps toward the bus stop when her arm was seized violently. Rad spun her around and shoved her in the direction of the parking lot, maintaining his visclike grip on her arm. She wanted to scream and scratch and claw her way free, but she knew it was useless. She submitted weakly as he propelled her to his car.

Rad didn't start the motor immediately. He stared instead at Lainie, who looked unblinkingly straight ahead. A peculiar numbness possessed her as she waited for the repercussions to start raining about her head. His hand reached out and turned her chin toward him, and the touch of his hand on her skin brought her senses to life, chasing away the numbness. Lainie moved backward to escape his touch before she dissolved into his arms.

"I believe you meant that," he said quietly. A blankness had come into his eyes when she had moved away from him. "But you ask the impossible. For the time being you might as well erase your mind of any thoughts about Lee Walters."

"Why did you come back into my life, Rad?" Her voice quivered uncontrollably.

"You were the one who came back into my life. You came to me for my help."

"You could have just given me the money and let me go."

"I could have," he agreed calmly. There was a scorching intentness in the way he studied her. "I probably would have if—"

"If what?" Lainie persisted.

Rad took her hand and slowly pulled her toward him, until she was nearly in his arms. Then he placed her hand underneath his overcoat against his blue-striped shirt. Unwillingly she felt the swift beat of his heart beneath her hand, contradicting his cool expression.

"If you still didn't have the ability to do this to me," he said. "You must be the original shrew, but this time I won't let you get under my skin."

She pulled away from him. And Rad didn't make any attempt to hold her. He seemed to accept the fact that their conversation was at an end. Lainie was hurt, confused and ashamed by the discovery that he had taken her back for physical reasons. Individually she meant nothing to him, yet nonetheless she still loved him. He was arrogant, cruel and callous, taking what he wanted from her and indifferent to any pain he was causing her.

This morning she had looked upon the desire he felt for her as a foothold to make their marriage work. The affection and love was all one-sided, and that tipped the scale against her. Lainie glanced out the window of the car, weaving in and out of traffic. She was reminded of her journey less than twenty-four hours before.

"Why aren't you living at our house anymore?" The question that had been unasked the night before came to the forefront.

"It was too big and inconvenient," he replied sharply. "I sold it about a year after you left."

"You sold it!"

"You surely didn't think I'd keep it for senti-
mental reasons? There were very few good things
that happened in that house." He glanced at her
cynically.

Lainie agreed, but she did so silently. What happiness they had known had been at the cabin in the
mountains where they had gone for their honeymoon. Love must have clouded her eyes, because
then her husband had appeared to be a very tender
and loving man, nothing like the embittered person beside her.

They arrived at the apartment building a few
minutes later. Rad unloaded her suitcases and
placed them on the pavement. She waited ex-
pectantly by the glass doors for him to accompany
her inside, but he walked back instead to the car.

"I have a couple of meetings to attend this afternoon," he tossed over his shoulder. "I'll be back
in time for dinner. Send Dickerson down for the
luggage."

CHAPTER SEVEN

IT WAS A LONG and uneventful afternoon. Lainie filled most of it with unpacking, arranging her clothes in the drawers allotted her by Mrs. Dudley. She called the hospital, discovered that Rad had already given them her change of address and phone number, and talked with her mother. Again she didn't mention that she was back with Rad, not finding any words to make it sound right. Finally she took a long relaxing bath, filling the tub with mounds of bubbles before finally dressing for dinner.

She chose a long skirt of black and gold plaid with a wide buckled belt at the waist, and wrapped several strands of long chains around her neck to complement the black turtleneck top. She spent nearly another hour in front of the mirror trying to decide how to style her hair. Her indecision stemmed from the desire to avoid meeting Rad again.

When she finally entered the living room, Lainie had chosen to sweep her hair on top of her head in a bun, a severe style that was harsh to her angular features. The evening paper was lying neatly folded on the coffee table—courtesy, no doubt, of Dickerson, Lainie thought irritatedly. She picked it up and leafed through it with desultory interest. Dickerson appeared almost instantly, offering her a glass of sherry, which she accepted. He informed her that dinner would be ready as soon as Mr. MacLeod had arrived home.

Rad came a few minutes later. He brushed away the sherry that Dickerson offered and walked immediately to the bar, where he mixed himself a martini. Lainie continued leafing through the newspaper, refusing to show undue interest in his arrival, even though her heart had increased its pace when he walked in the door.

"Have you settled in?" His voice came from behind the sofa where Lainie sat.

"Yes, thank you. How did your meetings go?" She refused to be drawn in by his baiting tone and kept her voice deliberately light.

"They were satisfactory enough, if you're really interested."

"Were you really interested whether I'd settled in or not?" Lainie snapped back.

"Unlike your duty question, I was interested."

"Why? Didn't you want to spend the evening alone?"

Lainie hated the tension inside of her that was causing her to be so sarcastic, but it seemed the only safe reaction to his presence.

"The evenings I spend alone are of my own choosing."

"How convenient to be a man and to be able to choose the company you want and when!"

"Yes, it is," Rad replied calmly. "I understand our dinner is ready. Are you ready to eat?"

He waited at the archway near the hall, plainly indicating that if Lainie didn't join him, he would go alone. She rose from the couch slowly and walked toward him, ignoring the impatient and demanding gaze in his eyes that ordered her to hurry.

"Arguing is bad for the digestion, so why don't we dispense with any conversation at the table?" he drawled just before they entered the dining room.

"That's an excellent suggestion, one that I heartily endorse." Lainie tried to make her voice match his stinging tone.

But the silence to her was uncomfortable, although it didn't seem to upset Rad a bit. The throbbing ache in her chest left little room for food. She should have been witty and charming, impressing Rad with her lighthearted conversation. Instead, the minute he had walked in the door that evening she had been bitchy and sarcastic. Why did they continually have to poke and prod at each other? There was that constant crackling of electricity between them, sparks generating more sparks. Lainie knew she had two options in front of her. One was to maintain the silence that Rad had decreed and she had agreed to, which would set a precedent for their future evenings together. Or she could break the silence with small talk and hope to set aside the antagonism and animosity that were riding on the surface. She chose the latter.

"I thought I would go to the hospital tomorrow morning," she said. "I'd like to speak to Doctor Henderson when he makes his morning rounds. And mother will expect me to spend time with her."

Rad lifted his eyebrow at the break in the silence. Lainie lowered her gaze to her plate, bracing herself for the sarcasm that would undoubtedly follow.

"You'll be needing a car," he said. "The keys for the Mercedes are on the hall table."

"I thought that was your car?"

"Of course it is. How else could I give it to you?" He smiled at her with an indulgent amusement.

"That's not what I meant." She was a trifle breathless, liking the way his eyes had caressed her softly.

"I have another car if you're concerned with my getting back and forth to the office."

"Actually, I *was* thinking about that." She smiled hesitantly.

"Well, you'll be needing transportation anyway. I believe Ann wanted to get together with you this week, too."

"You don't object?" Lainie immediately wished she hadn't said that. For a minute she saw the shutters start to close.

"I told you I wasn't going to make you a prisoner here." Rad glanced down at his plate thoughtfully before looking up at her with a sort of bland amusement. "But I would appreciate it if you wouldn't make any evening engagements without checking with me first. I wouldn't want them to conflict with any commitment I may have made."

"No, of course not," Lainie murmured in quick agreement, glad that she hadn't angered him with her question.

The meal was suddenly pleasant. The expertly prepared dishes had a better flavor. The chocolate mousse was delicately light and delicious. The whole mood seemed to have changed and Lainie basked in its warm glow. Later, in the living room, she was able to lean against the back of the sofa and relax in contentment as Rad put a stack of long-playing records on the stereo. The change in mood seemed to have affected him, as well. The lack of conversation between them brought an intimate silence, enhanced by melodious strains of violins in the background. A smile of happiness curved Lainie's mouth at the frown that gathered on Rad's forehead when Dickerson appeared in the archway, interrupting their privacy.

"What is it?" Rad asked sharply.

"Miss Gilbert is here to see you. She has some papers."

"At this hour?" Lainie exclaimed. Her smile

was replaced with a frown and she received a quelling look from Rad.

"I won't be long."

There was more than a fleck of green in her eyes as she watched Rad walk out of the room. Not if Sondra had anything to say about it, she thought ungenerously.

THE CLOCK TICKED past the nine, and the ten, and still Rad hadn't returned.

An inner compulsion drove her footsteps through the archway and on into the hallway, but Lainie was not even conscious of the movement. It was almost a waking version of sleepwalking. Not until she heard voices coming from behind a closed door did she realize she had left the living room. Even as she listened intently to what was being said, a terrible feeling of guilt knotted her stomach.

"It won't be long. A few months, no more." Rad's well-modulated voice came to Lainie clearly.

"It seems like such a long time, though." The feminine voice left Lainie in no doubt that Sondra was still there.

"Does it bother you?" Rad asked.

"Of course. Did you think it wouldn't?"

Rad made no reply to Sondra's question. Seconds ticked past and there was no further sound. Again Rad's voice broke the silence, but it was too low for Lainie to pick out the words. She reached for the doorknob. What did she hope to find in there? The image of Sondra's red head nestled under Rad's chin danced in her mind's eye, and she knew she didn't want to subject herself to the final humiliation of finding another woman in Rad's arms.

Her hand never reached the doorknob. She turned and walked swiftly back to the living room. This time she was thankful for the carpet that muffled her movements. Her fingers were twined tightly together as she tried to fight the terrible pain in her heart. She paused in front of the fireplace, half turning to let the harmony of the room soothe her restless spirit. The white, gray and black colors jumped out at her. They were a perfect backdrop for Sondra with her titian hair.

Lainie fled into the bedroom. Jealousy was a green flame that consumed the last vestiges of her hope. She stared at the bed, wondering if she could stand to have Rad make love to her again knowing that at the present moment he was consoling another woman. Slowly, mechanically, she began changing into her night clothes. Over the long nightgown of green cotton she slipped on a velvet dressing robe of olive green. Taking the bristled brush from the dressing table, she sat on the bed and began brushing her hair. The ritual of counting each stroke acted as a drug that numbed the pain.

When Rad walked into the room a few minutes later, Lainie was able to glance up at him with an aloofness she wouldn't have been capable of earlier. His tie had been removed and was sticking out of his pocket. There was a drawn tiredness about his face that made Lainie wonder with malicious satisfaction if he had perhaps had trouble reconciling Sondra to the change.

"I didn't think it would take so long," Rad said as he walked to his dresser and began emptying his pockets.

Her hairbrush swept through her hair with the one-hundredth stroke. Lainie rose from the bed, walking over to her own dressing table to place her brush with the rest of her vanity set. She didn't bother to comment on Rad's statement, her remoteness acting as a shield to protect herself from him.

"What's the matter with you?" Rad stood blocking her way to the bed.

"Nothing." She gazed up at him calmly, feeling like a mannequin devoid of any emotion and insulated from the glittering electricity in his gaze.

"There were some difficulties I had to get ironed out with Sondra." A light flickered in and out of Lainie's eyes at his statement. "Concerning business," he added darkly.

"You don't have to explain yourself to me, Rad."

"Don't I?" he sneered.

"Fidelity wasn't part of our bargain," she replied smoothly, sidestepping him and walking to the bed.

If she had been in a more sensitive state of mind she would have recognized the telltale warning signals being emitted from Rad. Instead of deriving satisfaction from hearing the way he slammed doors and drawers, she would have been frightened. Slipping out of her robe, she slid under the bedclothes, blind to the anger she had caused.

"Good night, Rad," she murmured as the light was switched off and the room was enveloped in darkness.

"Good night, hell!"

The sheets and blankets were stripped away from her. Lainie glanced up with a startled gasp, her hands moving up to ward off the naked chest that was descending on her. She would have screamed, but her mouth was covered by a punishing kiss. The euphoric sensitivity was gone.

LAINIE PUSHED HERSELF into an upright position, glancing around trying to identify the sound that had awakened her. Then she realized it was not a sound that had wakened her, but the cessation of a sound. Someone had turned off the shower in the adjoining bathroom. Lainie winced as she reached out for her olive green dressing robe to cover her nakedness. The bruise where Rad had buried his fingers in her arm was already turning a purplish hue.

As she slipped her arms into the sleeves of her robe and folded it around her, Lainie remembered how she had struggled to evade Rad last night. Her lips relived that avenging kiss that had ground them against her teeth. She had twisted and fought, pummeling his back with her fists in an attempt to writhe free of his crushing weight. But Rad had pinned her to the bed, not content until she had responded to his savage sweetness.

Her nightdress lay on the floor beside the bed. Lainie reached down and picked it up, examining the torn armhole and the ripped seams. A misty veil clouded her as she heard again Rad's husky voice as he nuzzled her earlobes, demanding, "Love me." It was an unnecessary order, since she already loved him more than she had ever thought possible. The torn nightdress was pressed to her lips while tears trickled down her cheeks.

"I didn't mean to wake you."

Rad stood in the doorway, a blue towel wrapped around his waist. Lainie turned quickly away from him, her blurred vision blocking out the way his eyes glittered darkly over her tear-stained cheeks.

"You didn't. Or at least, it was the shower. I'm not used to sleeping late in the morning anyway." The words rushed out to hide the disturbance of her heartbeat at the sight of his sparsely clad body. She wiped the tears from her cheeks. "If you're through, I think I'll take a shower."

Lainie attempted to scurry past him, but his hand shot out and grabbed the already bruised portion of her arm. A cry was unwillingly torn from her lips at the pain. Rad pulled the front of her robe open, pushing it over her shoulder to reveal the purpling mark. Lainie kept her lowered head turned away, knowing how hungrily her love-starved eyes would devour his face if she looked at him. He let her go abruptly, taking the nightdress from her clutching fingers, glancing briefly at the ragged tears before wadding it up and tossing it onto the bed with suppressed violence.

"I didn't mean that to happen," he growled.

Lainie pulled the green robe tightly around her neck, feeling a terrible coldness settling over her.

"Don't. Don't say any more," she begged softly. She loved him so desperately.

His fingers curled around her neck and his thumbs pushed her chin up so he could see her face. Her lashes were meshed together in tear-wet spikes that remained lowered over her hazel eyes.

"You said yesterday that I couldn't protect you from myself, but I will." His fingers tightened momentarily around her neck and just as quickly let her go. He turned briskly away from her. "There will not be a repetition of what happened last night."

"Rad, please—" The cry for him to reconsider was torn from her heart. Lainie didn't want to be denied those rapturous moments in his arms, the only times that she was the center of his world. It didn't matter what his reasons were for having her there.

"I'm not letting you go!" Rad exploded, mis-understanding the beginning of her cry. "The rest of our bargain stands."

"Why?" Lainie moaned helplessly.

"Because it amuses me," he laughed bitterly.

The hateful sound echoed in her ears as she fled to the adjoining bathroom and let the hot tears of shame and despair wash down her cheeks.

CHAPTER EIGHT

"DARLING, I'VE BEEN expecting you." Her mother's lips brushed Lainie's cheek in greeting. "You just missed Lawrence. He was here a minute ago."

"No, I didn't. I ran into Doctor Henderson in the hall." Lainie smiled. "You're certainly looking better."

"I've slept the night through without an ounce of pain," Mrs. Simmons beamed cheerfully. "A good night's rest does wonders."

"You're certainly looking better," Lainie repeated unconsciously, a terrible awkwardness taking hold of her.

"You already said that, Lainie." Her mother's laughter was like the clear, tinkling sound of a bell that was pleasing to the ear.

"I imagine it's because I'm so pleased that you do," Lainie recovered quickly.

"You really caused quite a stir around the hospital yesterday morning, didn't you?" her mother teased. A questioningly apprehensive look clouded Lainie's face. "I overheard the nurses talking about this incredibly handsome, fair-haired man who was running himself ragged trying to find you."

"That was Lee, I imagine. He was here yesterday." Her mother's clear blue eyes still had the ability to make her feel like a child, only telling half the story.

"You had the nurses green with envy, especially when Lee left alone and you left with a dark-haired man. I believe he was described as being devastatingly attractive by one nurse and elegant by another."

Lainie breathed in deeply, preparing to blurt out the entire story.

"I notice you're wearing your wedding ring again," her mother commented, watching as Lainie lightly touched the gold florentined band as if it were a talisman. "Which would mean that man was Rad."

"Yes, it was." Her hair was flung back over her shoulder with a quick toss of her head as Lainie braced herself to meet her mother's eyes squarely.

"You've seen him several times in the last few months, haven't you?"

"Yes."

"I thought something was bothering you, but I was too concerned with myself to care." There was a faint smile on her mother's lips. "But then I've spent most of my life with selfish thoughts."

"Do you mean that you don't object that I've gone back to Rad?" Lainie had expected a storm of protests and recriminations from her mother at her actions. This calm acceptance was something of a surprise.

"No," her mother sighed, for the first time breaking her gaze away from Lainie's face. "I think I'm glad."

"But I thought you never liked him?"

"I don't think I did. He isn't the type to stand for an interfering mother-in-law." Her mother leaned back against the pillow, gazing upward to the ceiling. "When you were first married, you were so happy and so radiant. Rad was the center of your world. Suddenly I didn't seem to matter anymore and I hated him for that. I remember your father used to take my hand and recite that nice old verse: 'My son's my son till he takes him a wife, but my daughter's my daughter the rest of her life.' He would assure me that Rad would soon have our house filled with grandchildren." Her eyes turned apologetically toward Lainie. "But I knew, the few times that your father brought up the subject in front of you and I watched you glance apprehensively at Rad, that I'd poisoned your mind in that direction."

Lainie lowered her head, not wanting to admit to her mother how much damage her advice had done.

"When you finally left him, I was glad. I thought I would have my baby girl back, but you ran off to Colorado Springs instead. Was I the reason? Did the things I said to you before you were married—were they the reason you left him?"

"They contributed, mother. They made me lose my trust in him. They weren't the cause, though, because they were things that could have been overcome. It was something entirely different," Lainie answered truthfully, knowing the discovery that Rad didn't love her was the real reason she had fled from him. She blinked at the tears gathering in her eyes. "I wish we could have talked like this before."

"So do I. But I was never a very good mother. I'm not a very good one now, because... Lainie, you didn't go back to him because of all the money we owe? You do still love him?"

"Yes, I love him very much." Her voice was choked by the terrible pain in her heart that knew how futile her love was. Lainie didn't resist as her mother drew her to her breast where she could cry away some of the ache.

HER HIGH-TOPPED, fur-trimmed boots picked their way through the slush near the edge of the pavement. White petal flakes of snow swirled lazily down onto the concrete pavement, while the leaden gray sky promised more than just a flurry. Lainie clutched the white-hooded parka around her neck as the dancing cold wind bit into her cheeks. Already shop windows were filled with Christmas decorations.

For Lainie, there was such irony in the gratitude she felt in this holiday celebration. Her mother's improvement had astonished the doctors, leading them to suggest that the treatments might have temporarily arrested the disease. Yet much of her mother's happiness was based on the belief that her daughter had at last found happiness. Her mother had confided that she had believed she had been the cause of their first breakup; and that their reconciliation was the greatest gift Lainie could have given her. With that knowledge, there was no way that Lainie could allow her mother to discover that her relationship with Rad was anything but perfect.

Rad had kept his word. He had left Lainie strictly alone. Mrs. Dudley had been instructed to remove his clothes to the guest bedroom, which did little to improve the strained relationship between Lainie and the housekeeper. Rad and Lainie still had their evening meals together, and there were no more late-night visits from Sondra, but a remoteness settled over their conversations that precluded even the opportunity for barbed exchanges.

There were many cocktail parties and business dinners, as Rad had told her, most of them taking place on the weekends. Like everything else, these parties were a mixed blessing. They took up time and allowed Lainie to be near Rad, but never alone with him.

Tonight was the occasion for another party, and Lainie had purchased a dress she had intended to wear that evening. There were some alterations to be done and it was to be ready this afternoon, which was the reason she had come into town.

A familiar voice pierced through the din of bustling traffic. Lainie glanced around and saw Lee Walters taking his leave of another man. She hesitated, debating whether to hurry by as if she hadn't seen him, but that opportunity was taken from her as Lee sighted her.

He walked toward her slowly, each of them murmuring a quiet greeting as he took her hands and drew her toward the sheltered opening of a shop front. His blue eyes studied her face hungrily.

"I've missed you," he said simply. "A thousand times I've picked up the telephone to call you before I remembered I had no right."

"You probably wouldn't have reached me. Between visiting my mother and attending various functions with Rad, I haven't been home much." Under the warmth of his charming smile and with snowflakes leaving white stars on his fair hair, Lainie realized how easy it was to be drawn into the undemanding affection of Lee—a situation she must avoid.

"Are you happy with Rad?"

"Life doesn't allow you to be happy all of the time. But most of the time I'm content, yes," Lainie answered truthfully. She was with Rad, his wife, and that was all she asked right now. "And you? How are things going with you?"

"My old man is slowly admitting that I do know something about business." There was no bitterness in his voice, only amused acceptance of what he couldn't change.

"You never have objected to working your way up, have you?"

"Occasionally—after all, I am human," Lee replied, smiling. "But I appreciate the lessons I've learned, too. Where are you going now? Could I buy you a drink, or a cup of coffee or something?"

Lainie pushed back her coat sleeve and glanced at the dainty watch on her wrist. "I'm afraid I don't have time. I have a dress to pick up that's being altered, then I have to dash home and get ready for another party at the Fredricksons' tonight."

"The Fredricksons?" Lee's face broke into a beaming smile. "I've been invited, too. That means I'll be seeing you again tonight."

"Yes, we'll be there." Lainie's deliberately placed emphasis on the "we" didn't cause the adoration in Lee's eyes to flicker.

He leaned down and brushed her cheek with a kiss, a boyish expression of shy delight lighting his face. Lainie lifted her hand in a goodbye wave as he walked away, then turned to retrace her steps to the department store. But as she turned she looked into a pair of green eyes glittering with smug triumph. Sondra was standing only a few feet away and had witnessed and heard Lainie's meeting with Lee. The girl stepped forward, her mouth opening to speak, as Lainie hurried past her.

LAINIE CAREFULLY SLIPPED the boldly colored apricot dress over her head. The dress was an excellent choice, its simply cut lines accenting her slim figure while the bright color enriched the highlights in her thick hair. As she smoothed the skirt over her thighs, she took pleasure in her own reflection. The superbly cut V neckline in the front made the dress appear modestly prim, but the plunging V neckline at the back made it appear daring. She put her hands behind her to zip up the back, only to feel the material catch in the zipper.

With a brief exclamation of disgust, she attempted to free it. The material was firmly caught and no amount of contortion could free it. Sighing heavily, she stepped out of the bedroom, calling for the housekeeper to come to her aid.

"She's busy just now. What was it you wanted?" Rad's sharp voice halted her footsteps.

"I didn't know you were home. You're early." He had caught her off guard and her surprise was evident in her expression.

"What did you want with Mrs. Dudley?"

"My dress—the zipper is stuck."

"I believe husbands can take care of minor details like that." The mockery in his voice was accompanied by a quirk of his eyebrow.

There was no way Lainie could deny his help. Her heart pounded in her ears and the blood rushed with surging warmth to her face. The fiery touch of his fingers against her bare back as he expertly worked the material free of the zipper turned her legs into quivering jelly. She yearned for him to put his arms around her waist and draw her back against the muscular hardness of his body. But as soon as the zipper was free, he zipped it to the top and secured the clasp. Then Rad moved away from her to the fireplace mantel where his drink awaited him.

"That dress is very attractive on you. Is it new?" he asked.

"Yes," Lainie murmured, secretly pleased that he had spared her a rare compliment.

"Is that what you planned to wear to the Fredricksons' tonight?"

Lainie's head lifted sharply at his extra emphasis on the word *planned*.

"Yes."

"Did you buy it specially for this party?"

Was she under attack? Lainie couldn't quite tell. His voice was almost too indifferent. "I bought it because my wardrobe is still limited. Isn't it suitable for tonight?"

"Yes, it's very suitable. It's too bad Walters won't be able to see you wearing it." This time the fire in his eyes glittered through his mask of cool indifference.

"Do you mean we're not going to the party tonight?" The trembling weakness left her, chased away by the anger growing inside her at his groundless implications.

"Does that disappoint you?" Rad sneered. "It certainly interferes with your plans to meet Walters this evening."

"What lies has Sondra been telling you? I accidentally met Lee in town this afternoon—I was going to pick up this dress from the dressmaker. I mentioned to him that we were going to the party at the Fredricksons' and he said he would see me there. I have no control over what Sondra may have read into it. Besides, you told me yourself this morning that we were going.''

"Our plans have been changed," Rad insisted.

"Well, it's certainly decent of you to let me know," Lainie retorted.

"I hardly had the opportunity, seeing that you've been gone all day." His voice was sharp, cutting off her indignant response. "I decided this morning that we would spend the weekend in Vail."

"Vail? Skiing?"

"Yes, I planned on getting some skiing in while we were there, but I have a construction project there that I want to check on, as well. We'll be leaving first thing in the morning."

Lainie hated it when he used that domineering tone on her.

"That doesn't explain why we aren't going to the party tonight."

The corner of Rad's mouth twitched involuntarily—Lainie couldn't tell whether it was in mockery or anger.

"I presumed you would need time to pack. And since you'll be away for a holiday, I thought you might want to contact your mother." Sarcasm convinced her that the twisted smile had been brought about by his irritation with her.

A hysterical bubble of laughter threatened to choke her throat. What had she thought? That Rad was jealous of Lee? To be jealous Rad would have to have some feeling toward her, but it was obvious that he didn't.

"If this is a business trip, then why are you taking me?" Childishly Lainie attempted to strike back.

"I thought it might be a diversion for you." Rad's smile held cynical amusement. "You can go or stay, whichever you want. It really won't make any difference to me."

A defeated dullness clouded her eyes. Lainie knew she shouldn't have expected any avowal from Rad that he wanted her with him.

"Where will we be staying?" she asked.

"Why?"

"I just wondered...I thought...." Her eyes took on a pleading look. "Isn't the cabin somewhere near Vail?"

"What cabin?"

Some words effectively close the door on further conversation and snap the tiny threads of hope. Rad's question was one of them. Lainie shrugged uselessly and retreated to her bedroom.

CHAPTER NINE

WITH THE RISING of the sun, the snow had ended.
All around was the evidence of its fall. Everything
was covered with a fresh blanket, pure and white
and glistening under the brilliant rays. Here and
there puffs of wind danced teasingly over the pow-
dery crystals, sending them swirling in the air only
to drift back to their heavier companion flakes on
the ground. Branches of the quaking aspen, barren
of leaves, were dressed in a wintry glaze of hoary
white while heavy white garlands adorned the evergreen branches of the conifers.

A sign poked its head out of a snowdrift made
larger by the deposits of a snowplow. A cap of
white snow dipped down, attempting to conceal
the words Loveland Pass. Ahead was the flashing
caution light of a snowplow patrolling the cleared
road. The white Mercedes edged into the next lane,
giving the yellow monster a wide berth as it passed.
For a moment they were enshrouded by its steamy
breath and the whirl and flurry of snow before
bursting through. The concrete path of the four-
lane divided highway stretched out in front of
them, briefly revealing its route. As they began

their descent, snow-covered outcroppings rose above them, snow clinging tenaciously to the boulders, falling away in places to reveal almost perpendicular rock faces. Ten miles or so farther on was the engineering feat called the Eisenhower Memorial Tunnel, its iron gray entrance leading to the other side of the mountain.

The chilling atmosphere in the car had nothing to do with the freezing temperature outside. Lainie wished that the serenity and peace of the wintry landscape before them would somehow transfer itself to her and Rad. When they had first left Denver, she had attempted conventional conversation, but his brisk replies had left her with the impression that Rad had regretted inviting her to accompany him. She couldn't keep her gaze from straying to his dark profile, its bleak coldness intensified by the winter scene outside the windows.

Without taking his eyes from the road ahead of them, Rad passed her a pack of cigarettes. "Light one for me," he ordered.

Lainie hesitated before finally placing a white filter tip to her lips. There was something so terribly intimate about lighting another person's cigarette. She did as she was told, passing the lit cigarette and the pack back to him. She watched as he placed it between his own lips and wondered if he could feel the warmth of hers. But with his impassive face, it was impossible to tell.

"Tomorrow I'll be tied up in a meeting with one of my engineers. I've made arrangements for you to stay with his wife, who's presently living in Vail—unless you'd rather spend the day by yourself?'' Rad spared her a cynical glance.

''No,'' Lainie sighed. What did it matter who he pawned her off on? Yet she couldn't help adding bitterly, ''How do you plan to dispose of me today?''

His dark eyes flashed with warning signals of anger.

''I thought I would exhaust you on the ski slopes this afternoon. Tiredness might dull the sharp edge of your tongue.''

''I only hope it improves your disposition,'' Lainie snapped back.

His hand wearily brushed the dark hair from his forehead. ''What do you expect me to do? Play the adoring lover? Even you know that would be pushing things too far.''

''I'd think it would come naturally to you, considering all the business trips you've taken with Sondra.'' Lainie's chin quivered at his unnecessary reminder that he cared nothing for her.

''Get it all out of your system!'' Rad glared at her coldly.

He leaned back against the bucket seat, inhaling deeply and flexing his fingers, which had been clutching the steering wheel. Lainie was stunned by the genuine weariness in his face and eyes.

''For the past month,'' Rad went on more quietly, ''it's been a round of business and parties and a few snatched hours of sleep. I know you're bitter about being dragged away from your precious Lee Walters, but since you're here, at least pretend to enjoy yourself. For a few days let's forget the past, the future and everything else.''

She felt his eyes rest on her thoughtfully, but she didn't glance over to meet them.

''Is it a deal?''

The coaxing tone of his voice brought a whispering agreement from Lainie.

RAD'S APARTMENT couldn't begin to compare with the luxury and elegance of his city dwelling. Yet the decor was in keeping with the rugged surroundings of the Rocky Mountains. The walls were paneled in oak and the shaggy carpet was a warm shade of persimmon. A faded brick fireplace dominated the small living room with its overstuffed sofas and chairs in warm reds and yellows, a startling contrast to the blinding white snowscape outside the picture windows. Here there was no staff to keep things running smoothly—not that the one bedroom and smaller guest bedroom, or the living room and the compact kitchen with its adjoining breakfast nook, would require one.

Rad did not give Lainie much of an opportunity to explore her temporary quarters. He carried her luggage to the larger bedroom and his to the guest bedroom, declining her offer to unpack his things. His calmly worded request that she unpack, change and be ready to leave for the ski slopes in an hour had only the barest ring of command in it.

Three-quarters of an hour later, Lainie joined him in the living room dressed in her ski suit of honey gold with slashes and stripes of chocolate brown. Rad, in a suit of black and white, seemed unappreciative of her promptness, nodding briskly at her when she entered and immediately escorting her to the door. His impatience was marked. He seemed in a hurry to escape the confines of civilization and pit his skill and strength against the mountains of snow. After his declaration that this was to be a weekend of relaxation, Lainie had thought his air of aloofness would disappear, but all the while his gaze rested brightly on the distant slopes.

Later, as they rode the chair lift to the top of the mountain, Lainie realized that she had wistfully hoped that they would recapture those last moments of their honeymoon spent here in these rugged mountains. It was a ridiculous wish, one that required the effort of two people to fulfill. And Rad didn't care.

It was in this state of apathy that Lainie followed Rad on his run down the mountain. At first her eyes studied the black figure in front of her, admiring the litheness and skill in his movements. Then the mountain demanded the use of her own muscles, which had lain dormant for over a year, and her own skill automatically returned.

The cold mountain air blew over her face and tugged at her long hair caught in a clip at the back of her neck. The yellow goggles she wore brushed everything with a golden hue. Her lethargy was giving way to the exhilaration of the moment. She dug her sticks into the snow beneath her as she listened to the swishing sound of her own skis. She saw Rad at the bottom of the slope watching her finish her run, and instinctively she kicked a ski out, jumped and turned to come to a stop at a right angle to the slope.

As she slipped the goggles on top of her head, her eyes were shining brightly. There was a cherry glow to her cheeks and to the tip of her nose. Her inhibitions were wiped away. Her mouth spread into a laughing smile as she looked into Rad's face. No more clouds were in his face, either—chased away by the intoxicating mountain air and the exhilaration of the sun.

"Do you want to catch your breath before going back up?" he asked.

"I'll rest on the chair lift," Lainie puffed, wondering how much of her breathlessness was due to the exertion and how much to the warmth of his smile.

Their second run was slower than the first. Rad no longer was at the head, content to slow his pace to Lainie's. Halfway down the mountain Rad stopped, took her hand when she did the same, and together they sidestepped up a rise. It was a small ridge that gave them a view, somewhat obstructed by trees, of both sides of the valley. On one side was the cleared run of the slopes, and on the other a forest of trees, fallen logs, a tangle of growth, and beautiful virgin snow. At the bottom of the valley a tiny mountain stream fought vainly to keep from being covered by snow, here and there disappearing altogether only to break free farther on.

"A Rocky Mountain high," Lainie breathed, and immediately felt embarrassed at expressing such a poetic thought. She glanced at Rad hesitantly through her veil of lashes.

But his face was directed toward the scenery. "Yes," he agreed quietly. "And a much more effective high than could ever be obtained from alcohol or drugs. Rocky Mountain high—lyrical but logical." He smiled down at her. "Are you ready to go again?"

She nodded and followed him as he made the traverse from the ridge back to the slope. They maintained a slow steady pace with Lainie taking a yard or so lead. She knew the cause of her lightheartedness was the sudden opening of the door of communication between them. Perhaps there was still something to be salvaged from their relationship.

She was standing upright on her skis, coasting down the slight gradient. She turned to ask Rad if they were going up again when her skis hit an uneven patch of snow and slid out from underneath her, and with unbelievable force she landed on her rump in the snow. For a moment she could only sit there, her arms keeping her propped upright trying to figure out what had happened. Then Rad was kneeling beside her, his laughing face staring into hers.

"Are you all right?"

Lainie had to give him credit for trying to keep the laughter out of his voice. She winced as she tried to shift her position.

"Who would ever believe that snow could be so hard!" She very tenderly rubbed the injured portion of her body.

"Which is injured, your dignity or your derriere?" he teased.

"The first is shattered and the second is bruised." Lainie shook her head ruefully, his bantering tone bringing color to her cheeks.

Rad's arm was around her waist to support her after she had scrambled ungracefully to her feet. She felt terribly awkward and gauche as she attempted to right her skis and finish the short distance to the bottom.

"We'll take it slow and easy while you still have something intact."

It didn't matter that he mocked her as long as she remained enveloped by his warm concern. Lainie was almost sorry when they reached the bottom, although she was beginning to feel the soreness set in. Rad glanced at her inquiringly.

"I think I'll sit out for a while," she said.

"You don't mind if I take another run, do you?"

"No, of course not," she said quickly. "I'll wait for you at the snack bar and indulge in a big mug of hot cocoa."

"All right then. I'll see you later."

He sketched her a small salute and headed toward the chair lift. It was just as well she was brought back to earth with such a bang, Lainie decided. She needed a level head to keep from revealing to Rad how much he meant to her. Although there was no doubt about it—a little bit of his charm was a heady thing.

Lainie couldn't stop her heart from jumping when nearly an hour later she saw Rad threading his way through the crowd of skiers toward her. The glances from admiring women made her just a little bit more proud as his hand rested possessively on her elbow and led her away from the throng. There was the contentment of a conqueror in his expression, as if he had just battled the mountain and won. Even if it was just the expansiveness of victory, Lainie liked the way his eyes dwelled softly on her face. For the moment it was enough.

She wasn't really conscious of where he was taking her. Not until she was led from the brightness of the outside into the darkness of a building did she take notice of where they were, and her eyes lifted in silent question to his face.

"Now that we've blown the cobwebs away," Rad smiled, "I thought we'd have a drink."

His smile, free of all traces of sarcasm and cynicism, gave sincerity to his words. Once Lainie's eyes had adjusted to the change of light, she found the lounge wasn't as dark as she had first thought. It was almost a picture postcard representation of a lounge at a ski resort, complete with a blazing fire in the fireplace and laughing people dressed in a variety of ski outfits.

"How are you feeling?" Rad asked as she gingerly lowered herself onto a chair.

"Fine," she said, shifting her weight so that it wouldn't be resting on the bruised portion.

Rad ordered hot buttered rum for each of them. The drinks arrived with swizzle sticks of cinnamon, and they sipped them appreciatively. The crowd in the lounge was too noisy to carry on a normal conversation. After they finished their drink Rad immediately suggested that they leave.

Twilight had cast its crimson glow on the snow-covered mountains. By the time they had stopped and eaten at a locally renowned restaurant and left, a blanket of stars covered the skies, accented by a shimmering pale half moon.

"Tired?" Lainie's long drawn out sigh as Rad stopped the car in front of the apartment prompted his question.

"No, satisfied." Lainie smiled at him serenely. Almost satisfied, her mind added silently, knowing that to complete the fulfillment of the day Rad would have to take her in his arms.

A nervous silence threatened to take over them as they entered the apartment, and she wanted to avoid that at any cost.

"Is there coffee in the kitchen?" she rushed in.

"Instant, I imagine," Rad shrugged.

"I'll make a pot. Why don't you start a fire in

the fireplace?'' Lainie was a little surprised by Rad's agreement to her suggestion. But then he was in an amiable mood.

Several minutes later they were both sitting in front of the fireplace sipping at the hot black coffee. Yellow flames licked hungrily over the logs in the fireplace, snapping and crackling as if smacking their lips over their woody morsels. Rad had not bothered to turn on any other lights in the room and the atmosphere was one of quiet intimacy.

''Tell me about this couple we're meeting tomorrow.'' Lainie forced her eyes away from the hypnotic flames.

''The Hansons?'' Although Rad responded, he continued to stare into the fire. ''Steve Hanson and I went to college together. I was the best man at his wedding after he graduated. He accepted a position with our firm, which at the time was my father's and his partner's. And since I did the same, we naturally saw a lot of each other.''

''I don't recall you ever mentioning him.''

''When we were married, Steve was in Louisiana handling the construction of a large refinery.'' Surprisingly there was no bitterness in Rad's voice when he referred to their own marriage. ''Their third child was born in Louisiana.''

''How many do they have?''

''Four. Three girls and one boy, the boy being the youngest. He's my godchild.'' He glanced over at Lainie and smiled. ''Sean is four, and more of a live wire you'll never find. When he was two, I invariably came out of any meetings with teeth marks. At three, he was always kicking my shins. Linda tells me—that's Steve's wife—that he's on a cowboy and Indian kick now. That probably means I'll be scalped this time.''

Lainie laughed and was delighted by this side of Rad that she had never seen.

"Do you know, that's the first time I remember hearing you laugh?'' Rad stared at her, searching her face with a thoroughness that left her breathless. "Ignoring those polite sounds you made at various parties, this is the first time I've heard genuine laughter from you in all these weeks.''

Lainie didn't know how to reply because she knew that what he said was true. He stood up and offered her his hand. She joined him, letting her hand remain in his for as long as he wanted.

"It's getting late,'' he said. "You must be tired and a little worn-out. Why don't you go on to bed?''

"Rad.'' His name was an aching sound that came from her heart. She swayed closer to him. He released her hand and shook his head negatively.

A little smile of regret lifted the corners of his mouth as he bent forward and brushed her lips lightly with a kiss. "Go on to bed—this time.''

Lainie did as she was told, basking in the warm glow of his half promise.

CHAPTER TEN

STEVE HANSON was about the same height as Rad, only more stockily built. His hair was fine, straight, the color of corn silk, falling across his tanned forehead. His wife, Linda, was much shorter with ash blond hair that had a tendency to curl.

After Rad had made the introductions, he and Steve lingered at the Hanson's apartment, which gave Lainie the opportunity to become better acquainted with Linda before she was deserted by Rad. She was anxious to become friends with this couple who were so obviously close to her husband. Although Linda was a quiet person, she was not shy. In a very few minutes their conversation lost the strain of strangeness and came easily to both of them. At that point Rad and Steve took their leave, Rad promising Linda that he would have her husband back to her that afternoon.

The Hansons' two older girls were off at a skiing party and their seven-year-old was staying at a friend's house, which only left Sean, Rad's godchild, at home.

He spent most of the morning dashing in and

out of the apartment keeping his mother up-to-date on the progress of his snowman. His hair was fine and straight, the color of his father's. The cold had brought cherry patches to his cheeks and button nose, yet there was nothing cherubic about his face or the perpetually burning light in his bright eyes. Heavy winter clothing hid the wiriness of his little body.

Linda kept Lainie laughing all morning with anecdotes of her son's mischievousness. Shortly after lunch, Linda was able to convince her whirlwind son to take a short nap while she and Lainie relaxed over a cup of coffee. The quietness of the apartment seemed to call for more serious conversation and Linda was the one to begin it.

"Well, tell me all about you and Rad."

The request flustered Lainie. She didn't feel secure enough in the budding friendship to confide the exact status of their marriage. "There really isn't much to tell."

"How long have you two known each other, then?" Linda wasn't a bit put off by Lainie's ambiguous answer.

"I met him six years ago," Lainie admitted.

"You must have known his first wife!" Linda exclaimed. "Steve and I were in Louisiana, so we never got to meet her."

Lainie was so stunned by this stat ment that for a moment she couldn't speak. She remembered then that Rad had only introduced her as

"Lainie." He had made no mention that she was his wife.

"Yes, I know her," she answered not meeting Linda's eyes.

"She always sounded like a spoiled socialite to me," Linda sighed. "Of course, Rad picked a rotten time to marry anyway."

"What do you mean?"

"Well, his father was just buying out his partner's interest in the business when he met this girl. He knew his father's takeover would mean extra work and responsibility for himself, so he opted for a quick marriage. In a way, I kind of felt sorry for the girl," Linda went on. "Here Rad rushes her off her feet, spends every available hour with her before they were married, and then after they were married he had to practically desert her for business. Rad's not like Steve, who's always bringing the business home with him. It must have been a difficult adjustment for his wife."

"Yes, I'm sure it was," Lainie agreed, discovering for the first time the cause of Rad's immersion in the business after they were married.

"Of course, when his marriage broke up he became awfully bitter. Today, with you, was the first time I recall seeing any softness in his face, except where the children are concerned. He adores Sean."

"What about his secretary?" Lainie couldn't resist the question. Sondra had always been the cause of most of her jealousy.

"Sondra the siren? I used to tease him something terrible about her." Linda laughed. Her blue eyes gave Lainie a sideways glance. "I don't think you have any reason to be jealous of her. If she was anything more than just a secretary, I'm sure Rad would have told Steve, and you can bet I would have wormed it out of Steve. I'm not saying Sondra wouldn't like it to be more."

Lainie took a deep breath, wondering how much difference it would have made if she had only known Linda years ago. "Do you think—" she swallowed to take the huskiness out of her voice "—Rad loved his wife?"

"I don't know. He won't talk about her. I can't imagine him marrying anybody he didn't care about a lot, but I wouldn't worry about that if I were you." Linda smiled at her reassuringly. "It's all water under the bridge, so to speak. Besides, Rad isn't the type to make the same mistake twice with the same person. Whoever she was, I can't see Rad taking her back again."

That statement only made Lainie more curious. He had taken her back, only doubt was forming that revenge had really been his motive. Deftly Lainie maneuvered the conversation to other channels.

IT WAS NEARLY three o'clock before Sean, who was only going to rest his eyes, finally awoke from his nap. After restocking his supply of energy with a tall glass of milk and four biscuits, he was ready to

return to his task of completing his snowman.
Linda was preparing a roast for the evening meal,
so Lainie volunteered to help Sean bundle himself
up in his winter coat.

"How many children do you have?" Sean inquired boldly as Lainie expertly tucked his muffler
inside his parka.

"I don't have any. But I hope to someday."
Lainie smiled at him.

"How many do you want?"

"Three sounds like a good number to me."

"All boys," Sean announced firmly.

"Actually I thought two boys and a girl would
be nice," Lainie replied solemnly, and heard
Linda's slight chuckle behind her.

"Yes, that would be all right." Sean had hesitated slightly before agreeing. Then his bright eyes
looked beyond her and his face broke into a beaming smile. "Uncle Rad!" he cried, hurtling himself
past Lainie.

Lainie turned with a start. Rad was standing
in the doorway, looking down at her with more
than just amusement in his eyes. Color rushed to
her cheeks and she was glad when the demanding
Sean captured Rad's attention. She took the
opportunity to escape to the kitchen where she
immediately offered her help to Linda, who handed her a bunch of carrots and a peeler. Lainie was
briskly shaving off the outer skin of the orange
root when Rad's hands took hold of her upper
arms.

"Are you glad to see me?" he whispered in her hair.

Lainie was saved from replying by Steve's voice calling, "Rad, there's a phone call for you. It's long distance."

Rad sighed, squeezed Lainie's shoulders and walked into the living room. By the time he returned, the roast, complete with carrots, potatoes, and onions, had already been placed in the oven. Lainie smiled at him hesitantly when he walked into the room, but his expression was grim and unyielding.

"I'm sorry, Linda, but Lainie and I are going to have to beg off our dinner date. Something's come up and we'll have to leave," he said tersely.

"What's wrong?" Linda asked, speaking the words that were uppermost in Lainie's mind.

His answer was directed to Lainie. "It was the hospital. They've been trying to get hold of us. Your mother's had a relapse and they want us to come as quickly as we can."

Lainie knew she must have paled. His arm came out immediately, supporting her waist when she faltered a step toward him. She nodded at the words of sympathy expressed by Linda and Steve, but her movements were guided by Rad, who was quickly maneuvering her toward the door and on to the car.

The trip back to Denver was a nightmare. But Lainie didn't allow herself to lose control. The occasional reassuring glances from Rad were of immeasurable help. As they mounted the hospital steps, Lainie was amazed to see a familiar figure rushing toward her.

"I called Ann before we left," Rad said quietly, "I thought you would like to have her here."

So it was in Ann's company that Lainie arrived at her mother's room. Rad was off to consult the doctors. It was so strange, Lainie thought, staring down at her mother. At one time she would have believed that her mother had deliberately brought on the attack in a desire to have Lainie at her side. But the new understanding and closeness that had joined them together in the recent weeks no longer made that true.

"The nurse told me earlier," Ann whispered, "that she was showing signs of improvement."

Lainie could only nod at that statement and pray that it was true. "How long has she been unconscious?"

"She's not really unconscious," Ann explained. "The nurse told me it was more a form of drugged sleep."

As if on cue, Mrs. Simmons's eyes fluttered open. Lainie walked around the bed and sat next to her mother, taking her hand. The dull blue eyes focused on her.

"Lainie?"

"Yes, mother, I'm here. Everything's going to be all right."

"I told them not to call you back." Her speech

was slurred and weak. "I wanted you to have the time with Rad."

"Sssh, don't try to talk. Just rest and get better."

"Yes, I will." Her eyelids fluttered shut again, only to pop open. "I'm not going to die this time, so don't you be worrying about me."

"I won't." There was a suggestion of a smile on her mother's lips as she again closed her eyes, and in seconds she was asleep. Lainie felt Ann's hand touch her shoulder. She breathed in deeply and turned to smile at her friend.

"She was reassuring me," Lainie explained.

"Why don't we go to the waiting room down the corridor?" Ann suggested. "I'm sure you could use some coffee and I know the nurses could spare us a cup of theirs. Besides, Rad should be coming anytime now to give us the verdict from the doctors."

Lainie nodded and accepted her friend's guiding hand. Walking down the corridor toward them was Lee Walters. They saw each other about the same moment.

"I called your apartment—" Lee looked sympathetically into her face "—and the housekeeper told me your mother wasn't well. I came just to let you know I was here if you needed me."

"That was kind of you." Lainie meant what she said, but she discovered that she wished Lee hadn't come. "Actually she's much better."

"I'm glad for you."

Lee would have gone on, but Lainie interrupted him briskly, "If you would excuse me, Lee, Ann and I were just going to meet my husband. He's been talking with the doctors."

Lee stiffened and stepped aside. Lainie felt Ann's bemused eyes studying her. She probably had been too sharp with Lee, but the truth was she wanted to see Rad—and not just because of her mother, either. Lainie recognized his dark form standing by the nurses' office. He turned at their approach, his expression hard. Lainie couldn't help the hurt from leaping into her eyes. She wanted to see the softness and concern that had been there earlier.

She examined the dark depths of his eyes, trying to find the warmth behind the coldness. If there was any, she couldn't find it. Without any preamble Rad confirmed Lainie's previous optimistic statement that her mother was better. Lainie knew she had made some appropriate murmur of gratitude. Rad said he was going to make some phone calls, and Lainie reached out and placed a detaining hand on his arm, but the suggestion that he join them died on her lips at the hauteur on his face as he looked down at her restraining hand. She withdrew it quickly, and just as quickly turned away toward the waiting room where Ann was.

Silence descended on the waiting room so that not even the hot coffee could thaw its chilling oppression. For a time Ann respected Lainie's desire for no conversation, but gradually decision formed on her face. She walked over, removed the empty cup from Lainie's hand and sat down beside her.

"What's wrong?" she asked.

At first Lainie just shook her head, attempting to brush off the question. But Ann was having none of that.

"You might as well tell me. I'll get it out of you anyway," she insisted.

"Did you see the way he looked at me?" Lainie murmured, tears springing to her eyes. "It's all so futile!"

"Why did you ever have to run into him that night of the concert?"

"It was all inevitable, I think. Fate." Lainie's voice was choked with emotion as she studied her hand clenched tightly in her lap. "You can't love to order."

"Does he know you love him? Have you told him?" Ann's blue eyes mirrored the depths of her compassion for her friend.

"No. What good would it do? My life would just become more miserable for telling him."

A slight sound came from the doorway and Lainie glanced up to look into Rad's face. There was such chilling coldness and contempt in his eyes that she gasped at the sight. So now he knew. He had heard her admit that she loved him—and this was his reaction. Rad actually despised her. She half expected to hear his mocking laughter scorn her pitiable confession.

"I want to talk to you alone." His words were clipped and commanding, tinged with an arrogance that sliced to the bone.

Lainie's lips quivered as she steadfastly met his bitter gaze. Without a word Ann slipped from the room, knowing that no matter how much she wanted to stay, the confrontation was private. Lainie tensed herself, waiting for the barrage of scornful words that would cut away the last vestige of her pride, but Rad continued staring at her, letting his minute study of her face unnerve her further. She knew he was savoring his moment of triumph when he had finally brought her to her knees.

The suppressed violence with which he lit a cigarette surprised her. Lainie had the peculiar feeling that the anger was directed at himself and not at her. At last his gaze left her face as he strode impatiently into the room. There was the faintest look of uncertainty in his expression. It confused Lainie. The Rad she knew was never uncertain about anything.

"You can consider our bargain fulfilled," he snapped suddenly, turning his glittering eyes on her. "I'll maintain the cost of your mother's medical bills until...until it's no longer necessary. But you're free to go."

"Free?" Lainie repeated sadly. She would never be free of him because she loved him, and the chains of love weren't so easily removed.

"Yes, free! I'm giving you a divorce," he

growled harshly. His lips curled at the startled look on her face at his announcement. "It's what you've been wanting for over five years," he added sarcastically. "Now you can have it. I would appreciate it if you would change your name back to Simmons. I don't want to be reminded that there's an ex-Mrs. MacLeod walking around."

Lainie closed her eyes as a wave of excruciating pain washed through her. She swallowed to rid her throat of the painful lump. Rad wanted to wipe out all traces of her existence. He couldn't even spare her a small amount of room in his memory for their happier times. Had she been that unfair to him before that he could hate her so completely?

"I'll make arrangements for your things to be sent back to you," he went on when she failed to speak. His voice had lost some of the leashed fury.

"I'd rather handle it myself."

Lainie's voice managed to squeeze itself out through the tight lump in her throat. His piercing look questioned her statement, demanding with his old authority a reason for that request. She knew he would be amused if she told him that she didn't want to take the clothes she had so recently bought at his expense, so she seized on the first available lie that sprang to her lips.

"I don't know where I'll be staying."

Rad stared at her unblinkingly for several minutes, a cold mask on his face that froze the tears in her eyes. Then he turned his back to her and ran his fingers through his dark hair in a gesture of tiredness.

"My lawyers will contact you," he said. His harsh words wrenched at her heart, twisting it with unbelievable agony.

He was walking toward the door and Lainie knew he was walking out of her life forever. She tasted blood in her mouth where her teeth had bitten her lip. Unwillingly she called his name and saw him turn slowly back toward her. She rose hesitantly to her feet, forcing herself to look into the carved features.

"I wanted to thank you." Her voice was only a whisper.

"For a divorce?" he sneered. His eyes raked her contemptuously. "I'll be glad to get you out of my life!"

Her head recoiled as if he had struck her. "No, not for that." From somewhere she gathered the strength to continue. "For bringing me back here today when mother was so ill."

He exhaled slowly, his shoulders sagging only slightly, but enough for Lainie to sense the unrest her words had caused.

"I regret that I made that ridiculous statement that I would let you go when your mother died," he said slowly. There was the barest glimmer of sympathy in his otherwise bland eyes. "I'm glad for you that she's better."

Lainie nodded. "I didn't really think you would use her as a tool for your revenge."

A wry smile lifted the corners of his mouth in irony. "The Lord's revenge is much more punishing than a mere mortal's."

The truth of his words bowed Lainie's head as the tears blurred her eyes. Yes, she would have to live the rest of her life without Rad's love. When she lifted her head Rad was gone.

CHAPTER ELEVEN

Two DAYS PASSED before Lainie had the nerve to return to the apartment. Luckily Rad had left the suitcase she had packed for their stay in Vail, so that she had an ample change of clothes. Ann had been insistent that she stay with them, and Lainie had been too depressed to make much of an objection.

The knowledge that this time Rad was giving her a divorce hung like a heavy weight upon her shoulders, dragging her deeper until she no longer wanted to lift her head up, to make any pretense at all that she wanted to live. The last time they had been separated, five years ago, she hadn't known how deeply she loved him, and also, the question of divorce had been forcibly ruled out by Rad. But not anymore. He couldn't wait to get rid of her; now that he knew she loved him, his revenge was complete. Lainie slipped the key to the apartment into the lock, glad that she hadn't returned it to Rad that afternoon at the hospital. She had phoned Mrs. Dudley only an hour before to ensure that Rad wouldn't be home during the lunch hour and to notify the housekeeper that she would be arriving to pack her things. Lainie had been quick to refuse the woman's barely civil offer to help, asserting that she was capable of handling it by herself. But as her shaky legs carried her into the living room, she wondered whether she could.

She stared at the fireplace, remembering again the first time she had been there. She hated the room with sudden violence because it was here that she had realized that she still loved Rad. Clenching her lips tightly together so they wouldn't give rise to the sobs in her chest, she glanced at the envelope in her hand. Before her resolve could weaken she slipped the apartment key inside, hearing the metal clink against her wedding ring, which was already inside. Also inside was the terse note she had agonized over writing, trying to keep her emotions from creeping into those few short words. After several attempts at writing it she had finally settled on two noncommittal sentences, knowing that any statements of her love for him would be read with amusement.

Enclosed is the door key and my wedding ring. I have no further use for either.

Lainie

It seemed wrong that two short sentences could contain so much unspoken pain. Quickly Lainie placed the envelope on the mantelshelf, her eyes staring at Rad's name written on the front. She wiped the tears away from her eyes and scurried into the bedroom. The quicker she accomplished her packing, the sooner she would be able to leave.

She never realized how many clothes she had, nor how long it would take to pack them all. She didn't allow herself to admit that part of the reason was the unwilling memory of the two glorious nights she had spent in this room in Rad's arms. But it was there in the way her eyes caressed the pillow that had known his head. Finally, with tears burning the back of her eyes, she closed the last suitcase and set it on the floor. She spared one last look around the room, wondering if Rad would be able to walk in and not see the bare dressing table that had once held her belongings. Those thoughts only brought more pain, so she quickly picked up two suitcases and her handbag, and walked to the door.

Her vision was blurred by the unshed tears in her eyes as she walked into the living room. As before, her footsteps were muffled by the carpeting. Her hazel eyes blinked at the dark form sitting on the gray velvet sofa. The mist cleared, enabling her to focus on Rad. The pain of seeing him again seared through her with unbearable waves of agony, but she couldn't tear her gaze away from the man she loved.

In his left hand Lainie saw the terse note she had written him. He was gripping the white paper so hard that it was nearly crumpled in his hands. His dark head was bent and his shoulders hunched over the object in his other hand. Just for a mo-

ment Lainie caught a glimpse of her wedding band
before he hurled it from him across the room. The
violent action brought him to his feet and she was
staring incredulously into his face.

The rugged features were contorted with pain as
he stared back at her, his eyes red and haunted.
There were tears winding their way down his face.
Suddenly he was bristling with anger.

"What are you doing here?" he shouted. But
the savagery in his voice couldn't hide the pain
behind every word. Rad seemed to realize it and
sagged onto the couch, turning his head away from
her as if it were torture to look at her. "What difference does it make?"

The defeated tone of his voice brought a different ache into Lainie's heart.

"After all the hell I've put you through, I guess
you should have some victory." Rad was talking
like a man broken in two. A bitter laugh came
from somewhere deep inside him and it was filled
with self-contempt. "And to think that for five
years, I've tried to make sure you never knew I
loved you. I even went to humiliating pains to
make sure you believed I never did."

Rad turned his tortured eyes on her, drinking in
the bewildered expression on her face as if he were
dying from thirst.

"Oh, Lainie, I love you so much. Forgive me for
forcing you . . . for blackmailing you into being my
wife again," he begged in a hoarse whisper.

"Rad!" His name was an exultant bubble that burst gladly from Lainie.

"Don't pity me!" he shouted, rising to his feet as he changed from the beggar to the dominator. "I couldn't stand that!"

"Rad, no." Lainie moved to his side quickly. Her hand touched his arm when he turned away.

"Go!" he ordered. "I'm sure Walters is waiting for you—for you and your two boys and a girl!"

"Darling," Lainie breathed, and felt the constriction of his body at her words. "Lee isn't waiting for me. And certainly not for 'our' three children. As their future father, you might have something to say about it."

This time Rad turned and stared deeply into her face and the love light that shone out of her eyes. His hands reached up and gripped her shoulders with the fierceness of a man holding on to a lifeline. Lainie could still see the shadows of doubt in his dark eyes and in the harsh lines of disbelief on his face.

"It's you I love, Rad. I always have," she insisted.

He continued to stare at her, his gaze gradually softening as he read the affirmation in her face. A smile spread across his face.

"It is true," he whispered. "You do love me." He threw back his head and laughed. "I thought it was Lee you were admitting you loved when I overheard you talking in the hospital. I knew you'd just been with him in the corridor and Ann said she wished you'd never seen him at the concert.''

He drew her into his arms. He held her so tightly that Lainie could hardly breathe, but she didn't care a bit. She felt him shudder against her and knew he was thinking the same thing that she was.

"What fools we've been, darling," he whispered into her hair. "We nearly ruined our whole lives."

"But we didn't, Rad." Her hands reached up to his face, her fingers touching the remnants of tears on his cheeks. "We have the rest of it."

His mouth covered her lips in a kiss that was unbelievably tender. And though Lainie's eyes were closed, a rainbow seemed to be shining in the heavens, piercing the thunderclouds.

Harlequin Romance

change and be ready to leave for the ski slopes in
an hour had only the barest ring of command in it.